From fairy tales to modern legal tradition, society demands we love exclusively, even though many only find happiness with multiple partners. Linda finally confronts long neglected sexual needs when Phil forces himself on her in Chicago. But back in Portland, her husband's insistence on monogamy compels her to choose between his limitations and her own insatiable desires.

Korin Dushayl's work "unfolds with the assured touch of a best-selling mainstream author, seducing us into the lives of people with needs and agendas that find wings in the dark."
     Larry Brooks, author of *Story Physics* and *Story Engineering*

As a FemDom, I.G. Frederick knows first hand the beauty of symbiotic D/s relationships filled with love. As an observer she sees the many ways BDSM turns ugly. She writes about abusive and tragic interactions as Korin I. Dushayl.

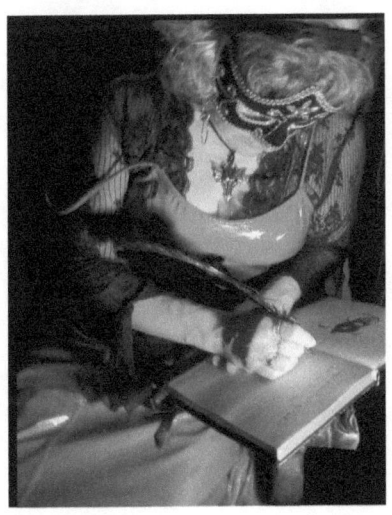

I.G. Frederick trades words for cash, specializing in erotic and transgressive fiction and poetry since 2001. Her erotic short stories appeared in Hustler Fantasies, Forum, Foreplay, and Desire Presents, as well as electronic, audio, and print anthologies. Her novels receive high praise from readers, critics, and other authors.

Ms. Frederick, owns the man she adores who although dominant in the rest of his life, demonstrates his love by serving as her submissive.

http://transgressivewriter.com

CHOICES

Must Linda's sexual awakening destroy her marriage?

KORIN DUSHAYL

Author of *Broken* and *Shattered*

Choices
First Edition
© **2013 by I.G. Frederick**

ISBN: 978-1-937471-89-7

Pussy Cat Press
http://pussycatpress.com/publisher.html/
P.O. Box 19764
Portland OR 97280

DEDICATION

To my college chum, Laurie, who stepped up
on short notice to provide the final copy edit.

CHAPTER ONE

The man pressing the entire stack on the weight machine stared at her. Linda ignored him and bumped up the speed on her treadmill, switching from fast walk to slow jog. She fixed her gaze on the television, but tuned out the chatter of the news anchors. Instead, she mentally reviewed the presentation she'd give in front of her boss' boss and the rest of the division in less than three hours. When the machine automatically slowed its speed twenty minutes later, she turned it off, figuring she could cool down on the way back to her hotel room.

Room service breakfast arrived precisely on time. She finished buttoning up her white silk blouse and opened the door. The waiter who set her tray on the small table rewarded her with an appreciative smile even before she added a tip and signed the voucher. Working at home saved a fortune in wardrobe expenses, but she enjoyed the opportunity to occasionally dress to impress.

Her phone rang while she reviewed printouts of her presentation slides over a mushroom omelet and sourdough toast. "Morning, Love. Did you sleep well?"

"You know I toss and turn when you're away from home."

She'd never known of anything that could disrupt Jason's ability to sleep, but the sentiment was sweet.

"Listen, you're probably getting ready to head to the office, but I wanted to let you know I saw an article on social media metrics and e-mailed you a link. Don't know if it will help..."

"Thanks, Love. The more ammunition I have the better. I'll check it as soon as I get to work."

"Hope it goes well. Love you."

"Love you, too." Linda ended the call and dropped the phone in her laptop case.

Tucking notes and printouts into her bag, she slipped on the tailored red jacket that matched her slimming straight skirt, ran her fingers through her short, curly black hair to make sure it was dry, and headed down to the lobby.

Stepping out into the withering heat just as the shuttle arrived, Linda noticed the man from the fitness center waiting at the curb. He turned aside to allow her to board. "Thought you looked familiar," he said with a wink as she slid into the seat behind the driver. "Phil Walker, Data Architecture, Seattle." He sat next to her and extended his hand.

"Linda Aaronson, Customer Service." She accepted his outstretched hand, but he turned hers palm side down and leaned over, bringing his lips close enough so she could feel their heat. She yanked her hand back and settled her computer case on her lap.

"From?"

She scowled. "Also from the Pacific Northwest."

"Do you like coming back East this time of year?"

She kept her tone cold, but if he was a colleague she couldn't indulge in her intense desire to tell him to go to hell. "I'm from Ohio. I don't consider Chicago back East."

He laughed, "When did you move West?"

"Late nineties." Since Phil obviously was determined to make small talk, Linda pulled her tablet out of her bag. She downloaded the link Jason sent while the driver negotiated heavy traffic, steering the half-full, twelve-passenger van from their hotel near the airport toward the sprawling headquarters campus in Elmhurst. The article gave her additional data points for her presentation, and she ignored the rest of Phil's questions to study it.

By the time she caught the shuttle back to her hotel, Linda only wanted to put her feet up, order room service, and talk to Jason. The exhilaration of successfully presenting to one hundred eighty-five people had dissipated as she participated in meeting after meeting after meeting throughout the day. Even lunch, a buffet in the board room, had been a meeting with her department managers. Tomorrow's schedule was just as intense and would end with no time to relax and only a few hours to sleep before she caught her crack-of-dawn flight home on Friday.

As the van pulled away, the driver stopped to pick up one more passenger. Linda placed her bag in the seat next to hers and leaned back into the plush leather even before she saw Phil the inquisitor climbing aboard.

"Mind if I sit here?" He braced himself on the seat back as the bus lurched forward.

"Yes, actually, I do." Linda didn't bother opening her eyes. "I'm wiped."

She felt Phil lean toward her and his breath against her ear. "I give a pretty mean foot massage."

Linda lifted her left hand in the general direction of his eyes. "Married."

"What does that have to do with one colleague helping out another?"

She felt his weight next to her and opened her eyes to see he now held her laptop case. She snatched it back.

"I'm off work. I just want to relax, *alone*, and get ready for tomorrow's meetings." She clutched her bag to her chest.

"Actually, I can help you with your project. I heard your presentation today. I've some ideas about how the company can improve its CRM databases that dovetail with your SM metric tracking."

Linda took a deep breath.

"Why don't we talk over dinner?" He leaned over and lowered his voice. "After, I'll make up for stealing you from your solitude by giving you a foot massage in the hot tub where we will be in full view of the rest of the guests."

She resisted rolling her eyes and decided not to claim she hadn't brought her swimsuit. Apparently, he accepted her not answering as acquiescence. When they climbed out of the van, he stated: "Meet you in the Mirage in half an hour."

Linda kicked off her pumps as soon as she reached her room. Even though they only had inch-and-a-half heels, her feet ached from standing on them most of the day. She stripped off her panty hose and washed the Chicago-area grime off her face. She wanted to change into jeans and slippers, but while she probably could have gotten away with that at a hotel restaurant in Portland, in Chicago one was still expected to dress "appropriately."

She settled for leaving her jacket in the room and slipping her bare feet into the comfy black ballet flats she wore while traveling.

She found Phil already seated in the center of one of the half-circle booths. Whichever side she chose she would have to sit next to him. She put her laptop bag on the curved bench between them and sat on his right side so she could wave her diamond and platinum wedding rings in his face.

Phil grasped the laptop case. "Here, let me move this out of your way."

Linda opened the zipper. "Not necessary. I want to have it available to refer to while we talk about CRM and social media."

"You don't want to spill food on your computer." He pulled it out of her hands and set it on the bench to his left. "I can always e-mail you any documentation you might find helpful."

She accepted the menu handed her by the waiter.

Phil perused the wine list. "Do you like white or red?"

"No thanks, I'm too tired. It'll put me to sleep."

The waiter asked, "Can I get you something to drink?"

"Ice tea, please." Linda handed him the dinner menu. "I'll have the onion au gratin soup and the garlic butter filet, medium rare."

"And for you, sir?"

"I'll take a cup of decaf, a Caesar salad, and the penne." Phil turned to Linda. "Too funny. They serve Seattle's Best coffee."

"I prefer Stumptown, myself. Tell me how you would improve our CRM?"

"I'd much rather find out how an Ohio girl ended up in Stumptown."

Linda waved her left hand under his nose. "I got married. We really do need a way to track SM metrics in the CRM database. Can you make that happen?"

"Of course. So, how did you meet your husband?"

Linda added two packets of sugar to the glass the waiter set in front of her and held her hand over the lemon while she squeezed it dry. "I've developed some spreadsheets that my people use to track their interactions with customers and prospects."

Phil offered her the bread basket and extracted a dark roll when she waved it away. "Did you have a long distance relationship for a while or did you just take the plunge and move across the country?" He buttered the roll.

"The spreadsheets don't integrate with the CRM. We have no way to incorporate the data except in the notes field, which is useless, of course."

"How long have you been married?"

Linda tilted her head. "Databases. That was supposed to be the topic of conversation."

He brandished his half eaten roll. "We've been working all day. Can't we talk about something else besides business, at least over dinner?"

The waiter delivered their soup and salad. Although the soup was mediocre, Linda devoured it. She hadn't realized she was ravenous until the scent of onions and Parmesan steamed up from her bowl.

Phil continued to ask personal questions, despite her refusal to answer them. She tipped her bowl, scraped out the last of the soupy bread, and slid out of the booth just as the waiter arrived with dinner plates held in cloth napkins. "I'll take mine to go, please." She stepped around and grabbed her laptop. "I only joined you because you said you wanted to talk about work."

Phil reached for the case, but she slipped it off the bench toward the floor and then pulled it to her, evading his grasp. After signing for her meal, she hurried toward the elevator, her case over her shoulder, balancing the take-away container and napkin-wrapped tableware in one hand so she could keep her room key in the other.

When she reached the fifth floor, she turned left, went half way down the hall, and waited. When the elevator didn't return, she ducked into the stairwell, walked down one flight, and passed the elevator to get to her room. Inside she put chain and latch in place before setting her dinner on the table and kicking off her shoes. She collapsed into the plush corner chair and dialed Jason on her cell before opening the take-away container.

"Hey, Love, how's it going back there?"

She smiled at the comforting sound of his deep voice. "Not bad. My boss really liked my presentation and so did the V.P." Linda unrolled the napkin. "Thanks for sending that article, those numbers helped."

"Fabulous. And, you'll be happy to know I finally talked to Richard about tenure again."

Linda sliced off a hunk of the steak. "And?"

"First time he didn't ignore the question. Said I could apply at end of term."

She swallowed a mouthful. "Think he'll support you?"

"No telling, but this is the most positive response I've gotten from him in three years."

She managed to get an "Mmm hmmm" through while chewing her second bite. Talking to Jason restored her appetite and she wished he were sitting across from her so she could rest her feet on his knee and cuddle with him after dinner. But then, if she were with him he would have found her something tastier to eat than overcooked steak with barely a hint of garlic.

"Tomorrow going to be any easier on you?"

Linda sighed. "Of course not. I have one-on-ones with my directs in the morning, then there's some sort of team building exercise all the afternoon. I'm guessing I won't get back here 'til after dinner."

"At least you'll be home for the weekend. Want me to get tickets for something?"

"Don't. I just want to stay home and relax. We can order take away and stream a movie." What she really wanted was to spend all day Saturday in bed making mad, passionate love to her husband, but she didn't want to say anything that would put him on the defensive.

"Your wish is my command, Love." He made a kissing sound. "I'll let you go so you can get some sleep. Call me when you get back tomorrow night."

Linda made a kissing sound. "Of course!"

In the morning, Linda waited just inside the second set of double doors that lead outside. She stayed there until the shuttle pulled up then dashed aboard. Phil followed her up the steps. He must have been waiting out of sight. She squished past a co-worker sitting on the aisle to take a window seat and opened the newspaper she'd retrieved from the front desk. Usually, she never read McPaper, rarely read anything in print, but it offered something to hide behind.

She managed to avoid Phil in her rush to get to her first meeting. After dinner, they had to queue up for the shuttles and Linda was lucky enough to get a seat on one of the first ones. She made short work of packing, but even skipping her workout she had less than four hours to sleep before getting dressed to check out and catch the shuttle to O'Hare.

CHAPTER TWO

When she walked out of the baggage claim doors at PDX, Linda felt dry for the first time since she'd hit the Chicago humidity four days ago. She only had to wait a few minutes for the Max red line and was walking home along Naito Parkway less than forty minutes later. She didn't miss Chicago traffic either.

In the building lobby, she set her roller bag upright while she emptied the mailbox. The September/October issue of *Cook's Illustrated* filled the small box and when she extracted it, a key fell out. Using it to open the larger parcel box, she found the white plastic envelope from the pharmacy. She smiled. They'd used up the last prescription early, splurging while on vacation at Crater Lake, and she was getting desperate.

Dragging her suitcase up the stairs, she realized how tired she was. Between the emotional tension of the past couple of days, walking the length of O'Hare, and too little sleep, she was exhausted. When she opened the condo door, a blast of cinnamon-scented air wafted out to greet her. She set the mail on the kitchen counter next to dish towel-covered plate.

Lifting the corner of the towel, she shook her head. Jason had an early class on Fridays. He must have gotten up to bake for her even before she dragged herself out of bed in Chicago, despite the two-hour time difference. Unable to resist the heavenly aromas, she washed some of the Chicago smut from her hands, pulled apart one of the cinnamon rolls, and let the yeasty, buttery dough melt on her tongue. Nothing like homemade treats to aid travel-fatigue recovery. Linda filled a plate and carried it out onto the deck.

Lounging in the warm sunshine, watching sailboats in the river, indulging in cinnamon decadence, she only had one wish. She pushed that traitorous thought away and concentrated on the sensuous flavors of Jason's culinary efforts.

Linda woke to find Jason covering her with a fleece throw.

He kissed her forehead. "Sorry, Love. Didn't mean to wake you, but it's getting chilly out."

She yawned. "What time is it?"

"Almost six. You hungry? Did you eat anything besides the cinnamon roll?" He pointed to the empty plate on the decking next to the lounger.

She shook her head. "Trip wiped me out. That was just scrumptious, by the way. What unholy hour of the morning did you crawl out of bed to make those?"

He smiled. "Not that early. I made them up last night so all I had to do this morning was stick them in the oven while I showered." He picked up the plate. "I also made chili and corn bread last night so you wouldn't have to wait for me to cook dinner. Figured you'd probably be hungry on Central time."

Linda nodded. "And after dinner?" She ran one hand up along his inner thigh, stopping just below his crotch.

"Since I did all the cooking last night, there won't be much in the way of clean up and I'll be yours to do with what you will." He winked.

For as long as the pill lasts, anyway. Aloud, she said, "Sounds lovely." She extended her hands and Jason helped her rise from the chaise.

After dinner, he loaded the dishwasher while she cut open the envelope, extracting the bottle with its meager supply. She left it on the counter and sauntered up the stairs, swaying her hips provocatively, smiling when the clattering of dishes ceased.

When she emerged from the bathroom, Jason had turned down the bed and stripped out of his clothing. "Don't you look luscious?"

She rewarded him with a smile.

"Give me five to brush my teeth." He disappeared into the bathroom and Linda stretched across the bed. The black negligee Jason had bought her for his birthday hugged her curves and barely contained her large breasts. The skirt flared out and she spread the satiny fabric across the sheet.

Jason returned smelling of mint and Irish Spring. He slid in next to her and pulled her into his arms. For a moment, she rested her cheek on his chest against the bristly hairs. He ran his hand along her right hip to her waist and dragged it up to her breast. With one finger he pulled away the fabric, licking her skin and covering her breast in kisses.

Linda moaned and moved closer. She tickled the soft skin of his glans, but he'd only taken his pill fifteen minutes ago. Jason worked his way to her nipple, sucked on it while one hand caressed her rear and the other held her left breast, squeezing it, and gently pinching the nipple, making her squirm. He pushed his knee between her legs so she could rub against it until she shuddered.

By then, she could feel him poking against her hip. She pulled the fabric of her nightgown up above her knees and lay back with her legs spread apart. Jason kissed his way from her breast to her thighs and probed between her legs until he buried his mouth in between her nether lips. Her hips rose to meet him and she sighed happily when his tongue found her clit.

He stayed engulfed in her folds until he had taken the edge off her need, then he kissed his way back up to her mouth. She welcomed his lips, covered with her own juices, and sucked his tongue into her mouth. Finally, he slipped inside of her and she moaned. He moved slowly, teasing her clit with pressure from his groin. She wrapped her legs around his back and pulled him in closer, shoving her hips up to meet his.

All too soon, he grunted and lay still, kissing her forehead. Although she had come several times herself, she was far from satisfied. She pressed her lips together to stifle a sigh when he rolled off her and gathered her in his arms. Nestling her head on his shoulder, she wished the pills worked better or at least lasted longer. She missed the younger, virile Jason.

Incredulous, Linda scrolled through screen shots and absolutely perfect report page samples. In the six weeks since they'd met, Phil hadn't contacted her once. But he had designed the ultimate plugin for incorporating SM metrics into the CRM database.

She picked up her phone and dialed the number in his sig, then hung up before pressing send. Instead, she hit the reply button on his e-mail.

Phil:

These look exactly right. How soon can you put them in place? Do we need authorization to add the modules to the CRM database, or can you just make it accessible only to my team?

Thanks so much for taking this project on. I know the feedback we'll get from collecting this data will prove invaluable, especially long term.

Sincerely,
Linda

She read the e-mail three times to make sure it was purely professional and sent it off.

The response came back before she logged off for lunch.

These are only ideas I had of what an SM plugin for the database might look like. I'd really need more detailed information from you before I could even start designing the architecture. I wanted to give you an idea of a look and feel I thought might work for you, but it's just something I pulled together in Power Point.

In order to build a plugin, I would need to know how many people would be using it, how often they would enter data, if you need data real time or can wait for generated reports, whether you want the reports just for your own information or plan to circulate them beyond your team, etc., etc., etc.

That's the kind of stuff I had hoped to talk with you about when we met for dinner last month. When will you be in Chicago again? Or, I could come down to Portland for an afternoon. Whatever works for you.
Phil

Linda put an index finger on either side of her nose and tried to rub away some of the tension. She really never wanted to be in the same room with the man again. If he came to Portland, they'd either have to meet at his hotel or in her home, and she couldn't permit that either.

But, her team desperately needed this plugin. She had to convince her boss, Sylvia, to approve another FTE she could dedicate to managing social media. But to do so required producing the data to justify moving social media from Marketing to Customer Service. She wrote back:

I'll be in Chicago for the quarterly announcements in two week. I haven't set up my schedule yet, except for the meeting of course. If you let me know your availability, I'll reserve a conference room so we can review specs."

The response made her shake her head and pinch the bridge of her nose, again.

I'm attending the meeting too, of course, but I'm afraid I'm booked solid the three days I'm in town. You'll just have to tolerate dinner with me at the hotel Wednesday or Thursday.

Nothing worse than a creep who has something you want. Linda made arrangements to have dinner with him Thursday night. Since she had an early flight Friday, she could always use that as an excuse to cut the meeting short.

Linda ordered the onion soup again and selected the penne à la Nicole as the menu item with the most potential garlic that didn't include shrimp. She decided to indulge in a glass of house red to calm her nerves. She waited until after Phil ordered his Chardonnay, so he wouldn't try to talk her into a full bottle.

"You never did tell me how you met your husband."

Linda took a sip of water. "The reason I need these reports, is to convince the V.P. that my department should manage SM, not marketing. I mean, have you seen our Twitter numbers? We should have ten times that, but they keep posting advertisements instead of engaging with customers and potential customers. My team only gets to respond to the tweets or Facebook posts that ask specific CS-related questions."

The waiter set her soup and Phil's salad in front of them. Linda stirred hers with her spoon, but resisted the tantalizing aroma so she wouldn't lose momentum or give Phil an opening. "If I had the data to show that CS interactions boosted followers and positive responses, I could..."

Phil pointed his salad fork at her. "I understand that part. But I work better with people I'm acquainted with socially as well as through business."

Linda sighed and scooped up a piece of soup-soaked bread with some of the cheese and onion in her broth. "I prefer to keep my business relation-ship on a professional level." She put the spoon in her mouth and watched Phil for his reaction to her statement.

His expression didn't change. "Database architecture works best if it's personalized, not only to the way its user will utilize the information, but also to the users' personalities. Otherwise, you're going to struggle with the interfaces and not get the results you want or need."

Linda took another mouthful of soup to avoid spitting out *bullshit* at the notion that he had to know anything about her marriage to design a basic database plugin. She debated sticking with her spreadsheet. But she really needed an interface that would allow any team member responding to a CS-related post to enter data about the interaction in real time.

"I've been married for almost twenty years, no kids, moved to Portland because he was going to grad school ,and he got a professorship at Portland State so we stayed." She paused for more soup.

Phil pushed his empty salad plate to the edge of the table. "How did you..."

She interrupted. "I've been with the company since I graduated college. Started out as an intern in marketing, hated it, loved the company, moved to CS in the nineties when they began offering telecommuting options."

The waiter set their entries in front of them and Linda took a bite of garlic bread, hoping her breath would keep Phil at bay. Then she realized he was eating shrimp DeJonghe. His might be worse than hers. But, why would anyone from the Pacific Northwest order seafood in Chicago.

"How did you two meet?"

She tilted her head and raised one eyebrow above the other. "Exactly why are you so obsessed with my marriage?" Her pasta had lost its flavor, but she chewed on it anyway, as much to avoid speaking again as to assuage her hunger.

Phil put down his own fork and leaned toward her just enough to be obvious, not enough to offend. "I'm not obsessed with your marriage. I'm obsessed with you."

She pushed to the edge of the booth, but Phil put his hand over hers. "Don't leave. I promise, I can deliver what you need from the CRM da-tabase. I just ask that you indulge me a tad by sharing who and what you are."

Linda sighed, but didn't rise. She pulled her plate closer and stirred her pasta with her fork. "I thought about attending grad school at PSU and visited the campus there. I met Jason in line at a nearby pizza place and," she shrugged her shoulders, "the rest as they say is history."

"Did you end up going to grad school?"

She shook her head. "I take courses periodically. I suppose I might have almost enough for a Master's if I bothered to pull it all together. But, I kind of lost interest when the company stopped automatic pay increases based on degrees. Mostly, I just take classes I find appealing when I have time."

"Can I interest you in dessert?" The waiter cleared their plates.

Linda stared at hers, not remembering when she'd finished.

Phil touched his napkin to his lips and returned it to his lap. "I'd love a piece of cheesecake."

"And, for the lady?"

"You have Tiramisu?"

"Yes, but we make it without liqueur."

Linda smiled. "That might be for the best."

"I'll be right back."

"Do you consider yourself happily married?"

"Yes." Linda decided to turn the tables. "And, what about you? Are you married?"

Phil's chin dropped almost to his chest. "My wife died three years ago. Melanoma."

Linda resisted an urge to reach out and pat his hand and wondered how he'd managed to engender such an impulse. "I'm sorry. Have you always lived in Seattle?"

"I miss her. And, I've never found anyone else who could..."

The waiter returned with their desserts and they were halfway through before Phil spoke again. Linda wasn't sure if she preferred the silence or his probing questions. Both made her uncomfortable.

"Yes, born and raised," he said.

It took her a minute to realize what question he was answering. Then she asked another. "How long have *you* been with the company?"

"Just since August. The day we introduced ourselves was my third. They courted me away from Microsoft even though I told them the one thing I wouldn't do is leave Seattle." He smiled.

"And you have the authority to develop plugins for the CRM database?" Linda scraped the last of the mascarpone off her plate.

"That's why they hired me. They want all the databases made more user friendly and better aligned to meet the needs of various teams."

"So, why do I need to have dinner with you to get my database needs met?"

"Because I've already got a list of projects that will take me a minimum of two years to complete. I'll probably end up doing yours on my days off."

But, only if I'm nice to you? Linda resisted asking him the question. He seemed to be implying that he would do her a favor if she would spend time with him. She hoped he didn't expect more than dinner because that's where she drew the line.

"Look, I've got some UI options you can play with loaded on my laptop. Why don't you come back to my room and we'll experiment so I have a better idea of how you'll use the plugin."

The waiter set the check folder in the center of the table.

Phil took it. "I'll take care of this. My expense account allows me to purchase meals for the employees I meet with." He signed the chit and Linda noticed that his room was only three doors away from hers. She hadn't seen him, even in the fitness center, since her arrival. He must not have invented his packed schedule for this trip.

"Why don't we just use the business center?"

"Have you been in there? Kind of stuffy."

"I'm sure we can manage." She smiled.

He shrugged. "If you don't want to come by tonight, we can wait until the next time we're both I town. I'll be back next month.

Linda sighed. Unless something changed drastically, she wasn't scheduled to return until next quarter's meeting. "Fine. Let's go then." She rose to her feet and waited for Phil to extract himself from the booth. At better than six feet tall, he towered over her. His powder blue shirt clung to a muscular chest and well-formed biceps and emphasized the blue of his eyes. She closed her eyes for a moment, then set her reservations aside and followed him to the elevator. The company had a zero tolerance policy for sexual harassment. Surely he wouldn't risk his job by behaving inappropriately?

CHAPTER THREE

The laptop sat invitingly on the table in his room and Phil pulled the arm chair up close for her to sit in. He stood behind her and pointed at the screen. "Okay, you just handled a CS request that came in via Twitter. Use this screen to log the information you want to capture. Don't worry about how you enter the data; the fields are more important for now than what you put into them."

The screen looked like one of the Power Point slides Phil had sent her, but the field names were blank. Linda tried to think of all the possible permutations of a SM encounter, named the fields, and entered the data.

Phil's cell danced across the table. He grabbed it. "Hi, Hon. Can I call you back in a couple of hours? You too." He set the phone back down and returned to his position just behind her chair.

"Thought you were a widower?"

"I have a girlfriend."

You sure don't act like it. Linda continued naming fields. When she sat back from the computer, Phil leaned over her shoulder. "Is that the order you want to be able to enter the data in?"

Linda reviewed her notes and nodded. "Pretty much. You could switch the ID with the customer number, and that has to be a field that's not required. But, other than that, I think this is the most logical pattern."

Phil turned the computer away from her and tapped a few keys. "Excellent, that's saved." He turned it back to her and stepped behind her again. "Now, would you have different data or order requirements for Facebook or Google? Are there any other sites you'd want to track?"

Linda reached for the back of her neck to rub the knots out. "Don't think so. Because of Twitter's character limitations, Facebook and Google will require fewer interactions. Except for that…" She shrugged.

Strong fingers gripped her shoulders. "Wow. You're tense. Let me see what I can do about that." Phil rubbed her shoulders, using his thumbs to get to the knots in her neck. Linda tried to push his fingers away, but he ignored the gesture and continued kneading her neck and shoulders. She didn't want him to stop, she realized. Her head dropped to her chest and she allowed it to flop around while Phil massaged out the tension that had accumulated since she left Portland two days ago. *He has a girlfriend. He's probably just a compulsive flirt.*

He leaned down and she felt his breath on her neck. "You should let me do more than your neck. Your muscles are unbelievably taut — I'll bet your blood pressure is through the roof."

Linda pushed at the chair arms trying to get to her feet. "I should leave. I have an early flight home."

Phil continued rubbing. "You'll sleep better if you let me help you relax."

"Really, I need to go."

"Why don't you get these clothes out of my way so I can give you a proper massage?" He ran one finger down her arm. "I'll go wait in the bathroom while you get undressed, if that will make you feel more comfortable."

"Sure." Since he wouldn't take no for an answer, Linda decided it best to leave when Phil closed the bathroom door. He pulled the blankets aside from half the bed, grabbed a towel from the bathroom, and tossed it on the sheets. "Here, cover your rear if you wish." He stepped inside and closed he door. "Call me when you're ready."

Linda was halfway across the room when her hand went up to her neck and she realized much of the tension that had settled in her shoulders was gone. She rubbed her knuckles into the small of her back. She hated traveling. As she'd accepted promotion after promotion and technology made it easier and easier to work with people long distance, her primary negotiation request had always been fewer trips to the corporate office. She stared at the bed. It took her a minute to realize her fingers were unbuttoning her blouse.

Fuck it. I need this. He's got a girlfriend and if he tries anything I can threaten to get him fired.

She draped her blouse over the chair she'd just vacated.

Don't be naïve. He only wants you naked for one reason.

She added her skirt and bra to the pile.

And the reality is that's the one part of me most in need of tension relief.

She lay down on her stomach and draped the towel across her backside from mid thigh to just above her crack, covering her panties. She settled her head on her folded arms. "Okay."

She heard the door open. The room lights, with the exception of the one on the night stand, clicked out one by one.

Phil sighed. "I hope your husband appreciates the gorgeous woman he's fortunate enough to have coming home to him tomorrow."

Warm, strong hands rubbed lotion into her shoulder blades. Slowly he kneaded away the tension from every inch of her back. The warmth of his hands, the fingers pressing into her muscles, the rose scent of the hotel's lotion smoothing her skin, lulled Linda into a hypnotic state. She was aware of the crisp linen sheets pressed against her belly, the hum of the room air conditioner, the heat of Phil's body and every motion of his hands. But, she was so relaxed, she could have drifted off to sleep in an instant.

"I don't think your back is the only thing that's tense." Phil's big hands turned her over on her back. *I can't. Jason.* She pulled at the towel to cover her breasts, turning it so she wouldn't expose her panties. "Thanks, that was lovely..."

Phil pulled down her panties and buried his head between her legs, draping her calves over his shoulders.

She pushed at his forehead. "Please, don't. What about your girlfriend?"

He instantly found her nub. She hadn't had sex in two weeks. The massage had turned her on more than she realized. She shuddered almost as soon as the tip of his hot moist tongue touched her clit.

"Please, stop." She put her heels on his shoulder, but he had his arms wrapped around her thighs and wouldn't budge.

"So tasty." He embraced her engorged clit with his lips while teasing it with his tongue.

She tried to roll to one side, to escape the exquisite torture, but she shuddered again, her entire body convulsing.

"Why? You promised?" *I'm so sorry, Jason. I should have left when I had the chance.*

"Promised what?" He kissed the inside of first one thigh and then the other, then her sticky mound. He pushed the towel away with his forehead and kissed her plump tummy, licking his way from her belly button to her breasts.

"Just a massage." *And, you didn't believe him.*

"But, how could any man resist such a delectable morsel. Your husband must ravage you several times daily."

A tear crept out of the corner of Linda's eye. "Please. I'm begging you. Please..."

He peeled the towel away from her breasts, easing it out from under arms clenched to her chest, and his mouth clamped onto one nipple. His big hand tried unsuccessfully to contain her other tit and he slid inside her before she realized he was naked.

"No!" She screamed. But, she came again, his cock, huge compared to Jason's, filling her, massaging her inside with the same pressure his fingers had applied to her back.

He chuckled and pushed his lips against hers, his tongue invading her mouth with ferocity equal to that of his cock plunging into her. He moved faster, harder, slamming into her, his pubes colliding with her clit, her tits flopping up and down, sending her into an orgasm that wouldn't end.

She kept her hands at her sides, her fists gripping bunches of sheet. But her body betrayed her, the intensity of her pleasure increasing with the savagery of his assault. Tears flowed down either side of her cheek into her ears.

When she feared she wouldn't survive another tremor, he groaned. He was so big, she could feel every spasm as he pumped her full of his seed. *Oh, Jason, what have I done to you?*

As soon as he rolled off her, she turned on her side, trying to extract herself from the bed, but he enfolded her in his arms. "You don't have to leave. You can spend the night here."

"Let me go. Why would I want to sleep with a rapist?"

"Don't be ridiculous. How many times did you come?" He imprisoned her, his chest pressed against her back, his arms and legs wrapped around her, his semi-hard cock pushing against her ass cheeks.

She didn't have the strength to break free. Her sobs shook her body almost as much as the orgasms had.

"Linda, what's wrong?"

"What's wrong?" *I betrayed the man who loves me, that's what's wrong.* Her anger gave her enough force to push his arms away, but he still had her thighs locked inside his own.

"You raped me!"

"Don't be ridiculous. You can't tell me you didn't enjoy that."

"I'm married. I told you no, over and over again."

He took a deep breath. "I'm sorry. You were enjoying it so much … I thought you were just saying no for propriety's sake."

His statement cut too close too the truth and her sobs cut off her breath.

One hand caressed her arm from wrist to shoulder. "If you weren't married would you be upset now?"

She gasped for breath. "Of course I would. I said no."

He kissed her neck. "But you came so many times. And, so hard. I very much enjoyed making you come."

One hand slid back around her and clutched her left tit. Even though she clenched her ample thighs together, he still managed to wiggle a finger between them and reach into her slit. She pushed at his forearms, but he tightened his grip. She tried to turn over onto her stomach to get away from the assault on her clit. He rubbed until she shook in his arms. Now fully erect, he used his knee to force her legs apart so he could slide into her moistness from behind.

"Stop." Linda squirmed, but arms like bands of steel kept her still. Phil's cock slammed over and over against her G-spot while his finger compressed her clit. She clenched her teeth, but couldn't stop the tension building between her legs from escalating until she shook in Phil's arms again. "Please." Her eyes hurt from crying and her nose was so stopped up she could only breathe through her mouth.

Phil squeezed her tit harder, dug into her clit with more pressure, and increased both the speed and force with which he slammed into her from behind. His balls slapped against her ass, his teeth sunk into her neck, he pinched her nipple between his thumb and forefinger.

"No more. Please, stop." Shuddering orgasms interrupted Linda's words. "Why?" She had never come so hard, so long, and so many times in one evening. But, she would have forgone them all not to be naked at this man's mercy, unable to move, unable to leave, unable to stop the assault on her senses and her marriage. *He's right. If I weren't married...*

When Phil finally came again and stopped moving, his softening cock still inside her, Linda's sobs shook them both more violently than her orgasms had.

"Wow. Never known a woman to come so many times before. Or react so splendidly after." Phil stroked her hair.

Linda wanted to vomit. "Splendidly? Do you enjoy feeling your victims suffer, seeing them cry, hearing them beg you to stop? Is that what turns you on, you sick fuck."

CHAPTER FOUR

The arms holding her in place relaxed just a bit and Linda pushed her way free of his grasp, tumbling off the bed onto the floor. He reached for her, but she grabbed her clothes and dashed into the bathroom, slamming the door and locking it in one motion.

Shaking, she wet one of the clean hand towels and wiped the stickiness from the inside of her thighs. She fumbled with bra hooks and skirt buttons trying to get dressed. One of her buttons popped off and she heard it bouncing on the tile floor but couldn't see where it went through the haze of tears. She hadn't retrieved her panties. When she finally got her blouse buttoned and her skirt straightened she dared to look in the mirror. Her eyes were red and puffy, tears streaked her skin, and her hair was matted to her head.

Her chin hit her chest. Her laptop bag was out in the room with her rapist. In it were her cell phone and room key, the only two ways she had out of here. Leaning her back against the door, she tried to stop shaking long enough to figure out what to do.

"Linda? Are you all right in there?"

She shook her head, even though she knew he couldn't see her.

"I'm going to order room service, what do you want?"

She shook her head again. She heard his voice muffled at first then at the door again. "Crap, they say it's too late to get delivery, I have to go pick it up. Don't go anywhere, I'll be back in ten. I think we need to talk."

Linda waited until she heard the room door open and close. She tore out of the bathroom, grabbed her bag, shoes, and panties, and ran to the door. She paused, pulled it open slowly, and peeked out into the hallway. When she saw it was empty, she dashed to her room. Shaking hands and card keys did not make a good combination, but she got the door open just as she heard the elevator ping. She slammed her room door closed behind herself.

With her door locked and latched, she finally felt safe. Almost. Phil still worked for the same company. She didn't know whether to call the police, wait until morning and call HR, or... The last thing she wanted to do was admit she had betrayed her husband by getting naked in a co-worker's room and letting him give her a massage. *But, I said no. Over and over, I said no.*

She sat on the bed, her head in her hands, shaking. She had no more tears. Still in her clothes, she dropped over on her side and fell asleep.

Her cellphone jangled her awake. The red numbers of the clock in the darkened room shone four a.m. She had two hours to get to the airport. If she called the police she would miss her flight and they would ask why she didn't call the night before, why she was in Phil's room, why she took off her clothing.

Sobbing again, Linda stripped off her clothes and turned on the shower. With a washcloth, she scrubbed and scrubbed between her legs, wondering if she could ever feel clean there again.

After toweling dry, she pulled on her jeans and stuffed everything in her suitcase. The bill and a hotel stationary envelope with her name handwritten on it were on the floor in front of the door. She added them to her laptop case, checked out using the television, and called the front desk to request a spot on the airport shuttle.

She made it through security with half an hour to spare, not long enough to bother booting up her computer and she didn't feel like doing anything on her tablet. Remembering the envelope, she extracted it from her bag. Inside was a letter, handwritten on the hotel stationary left in every room's desk. As she read it, Linda's hand shook so much the paper wavered in front of her eyes and she had trouble making out the words.

Beautiful Linda,

I am so very sorry you believe I took advantage of you last night and for my misreading your enjoyment of our sexual encounter for consent. My only excuse is that I am completely smitten with you — your voluptuous beauty, your raw sexual energy, your amazing ability to have orgasm after orgasm after orgasm.

If you never want to see me again, I will understand. I will still provide you with the database plugin you need, but I will force myself to do all work and communication with you via e-mail. I can promise you this because I will always have the memory of our one passionate night together to sustain me.

If you truly believe I raped you and you want to file charges, I will accept your decision, and I will plead guilty so you may avoid the embarrassment of a trial.

All my love,

Phil

She heard her flight called. Unsure whether to throw the letter away or keep it for evidence, Linda crammed it into her laptop bag. She'd used miles she had been saving to take Jason to Hawaii to upgrade to first class. As soon as she was seated, she ordered a scotch rocks. By the time the plane landed in Portland, she was tipsy enough to be grateful she hadn't parked her car at the airport, because she didn't think she was capable of driving home. Normally, if she didn't drive she just took the Max, but unsure she could negotiate light rail in her current state she grabbed a taxi.

When she arrived home, Linda left her luggage in the living room, went upstairs, stripped off her clothes, and took another shower. After toweling off, she slipped into a cotton nightgown and crawled into bed.

Weight pushing down her side of the bed woke Linda. The room was dark, and according to the red clock numbers it was seven in the evening.

"Are you okay, Sweetie?" Jason kissed her forehead and she relaxed. She knew she would always be safe with him. She tensed again when she remembered the previous night and tried to find the words to explain to her husband what had happened.

Jason ran his fingers through her curls. "When I came home and saw your suitcase in the middle of the living room, I figured the trip had worn you out. I made you some chicken soup."

She couldn't tell Jason, she realized. If she did, it would devastate him and probably destroy their marriage. How could she do that to him? Or to herself. Would she survive without him?

Linda forced herself to smile. "With dumplings?" Jason's idea of chicken soup was more like chicken stew, and it was one of her favorites among the myriad dishes he charmed her with every day, especially when he dropped in his fluffy buttermilk dumplings. He took perverse pleasure in adding dumplings with milk in them to his grandmother's otherwise kosher recipe.

"Of course, if only to make it *trafe*." He winked and rested the back of his fingers against her cheek. "Want to come down and have some or are you needing dinner in bed?"

She opened her arms. "It depends. Will you join me in bed?"

He scooped her up into his arms and nuzzled her neck with his lips. "If you want more than a dinner companion, you'll have to wait until the morning. It's been rather a stressful week here as well. But, my prescription came in today's mail."

"Tomorrow morning then. Consider it a date." Linda hugged him. "I guess I'll come down for dinner."

He helped her sit up. "Lovely. Why don't you get dressed and I'll go set the table."

When she descended the stairs, Linda was treated to the wonderful bouquet of chicken, onion, and garlic. The steaming bowl Jason set in front of her had big chunks of meat swimming in broth with celery, onions, potatoes, parsnips, and carrots. Soft, white dumplings floated on top. She inhaled deeply before dipping her spoon into the hearty soup and tried to enjoy it despite wishing they were upstairs in bed instead. She desperately needed Jason to erase her memories of the night before. "What time did you get home?"

Jason sat across from her and blew on a spoonful of stew. "Only about two hours ago. I put the soup in the slow cooker before I left this morning. Figured you were going to need a pick me up when you didn't call last night. I take it the team building stuff yesterday ran late?"

Linda lifted a spoonful to her lips, hiding behind the steam that rose to envelop her face. "Sorry I didn't call. I got almost no sleep as it was." If she reported Phil's rape, Jason couldn't blame her for what happened. She could count on him for comfort and support. Still, she had to tell him now.

But, she couldn't find the words to describe what happened, to explain how her body had reacted, how the intensity filled a long-ignored need. He would want to know why she took her clothes off, why she allowed a coworker give her a full-body massage. She knew the answer. *Because I don't get enough intimacy from you. And no amount of wonderful food will ever make up for only getting laid a couple of times a week at best.* She also knew she could never ever tell him that, either.

Jason tapped her bowl with his spoon. "Are you all right? You haven't heard a word I've said."

Linda shook her head. "Still tired. The soup's wonderful, as usual." She took another mouthful surprised to find it had cooled enough to not burn her lips. "I may just go back to bed to recover after I finish."

He put a hand on the one she had resting on the table. "I understand, Sweetie. Before you do, though, I popped in and picked up dessert from Cupcake Jones. I got your favorite, Lemoncello."

Linda forced herself to smile. She would put money on Jason stopping at the bakery before he went to school and reserving her first choice, since he would have picked it up just before they closed on his way home.

Which would shatter Jason's world more, she wondered, what happened or why? How could she even think about destroying this kind, considerate, loving man's heart by telling him what she had done? "Thanks, Sweetie. Lovely way to end a wretched week."

Linda stared at the e-mail and couldn't decide whether to delete it, forward it to her boss, or respond. Maybe she should mark it as spam so future mail from Phil would go to her junk folder.

Dearest Linda,

Since the cops haven't shown up to arrest me and I've traveled in and out of O'Hare without encountering any problems, I'm guessing you've decided not to pursue rape charges against me.

One reason could be you don't want the hassle of charging a co-worker. Another reason, the one I'm hoping is accurate, is that despite your tears and protestations, you really did want me to make love to you that night.

If the latter assessment is correct, you can contact me via my personal e-mail and/or telephone number.

After the contact information, he had the gall to sign it "Love, Phil."

Linda pushed away from her desk, went to the kitchen, and poured herself another cup of coffee. If she was completely honest with herself, she would have to admit how much she enjoyed sex with Phil. Even the way he took control of her appealed to something she had hidden from Jason, and from herself, all her adult life.

When she sat back down at her desk, she moved from the still open e-mail to her calendar. Then she hit respond.

Phil:
   I need to talk to you. Jason will be in San Francisco for a conference this weekend (Oct. 20-21). Can you come down?
Linda

She intentionally did not put "dear" in front of Phil or use anything but her name at the end. She even deliberately used a colon after "Phil" rather than the less formal comma.

For the rest of the week, Linda debated whether to meet Phil somewhere for lunch or just have him come by the condo. He told her he would arrive on the eleven fifteen train and her home in Old Town was less than a quarter mile from the station. The afternoon before Jason left for the Bay area, she still hadn't responded to his last e-mail asking where to meet her.

CHAPTER FIVE

"Doing anything this weekend?" Jason arranged slacks and sports shirts in a garment bag.

Linda crossed her arms under her breasts and gripped her biceps. "Probably not. Got a lot of catch up reading to do." She gritted her teeth, horrified by how easily she could invent lies to tell her husband.

"Work or pleasure?" He looked up and she frowned. "You really need to relax more."

She shrugged. "Maybe I'll take some time off and go out for lunch."

"Sounds like a great idea." He stuffed underwear and socks into one of the bags' interior pockets. "You work too much."

"This from a man spending his weekend at a conference in California?"

He folded the bag in half and clipped the sides together. "I only do this once or twice a year, and hearing papers and meeting with colleagues invigorates me." He faced her, his arms crossed over his chest, his expression stern. "I don't come back from my trips so worn out I spend the rest of the day in bed."

"Guilty." Of course, the real reason she spent the day in bed after her last trip was one she had resolved never to share with him. She refrained from reminding him that she earned half again as much as he did and without her salary, they couldn't afford their dream house on the edge of Old Town with a view of the river, close enough to PSU for him to walk to school.

Given how well they were known in the neighborhood, Linda decided it better not to risk having the conversation she planned where anyone who might know her could overhear. *Safer to have Phil come to the house.* She sent him the address.

He arrived just before noon. When she admitted him, she realized for the first time exactly how attractive he was. He smelled of leather and Old Spice shaving cream, such a contrast to Jason whose skin more often than not carried the odor of whatever he'd been cooking whether garlic or cinnamon.

She indicated one of the chairs at the oak dining table with one hand, while latching the door with the other. He set an overstuffed laptop bag on the floor by the door and stood in front of the seat she'd indicated.

He waited there until she sat opposite then lowered his muscular frame onto the padded seat. "Good to see you, beautiful."

"I suppose you call all your rape victims that?" Linda poured a herself cup from the thermos carafe. "Coffee?" She pushed it toward Phil then took a sip, letting the aroma of the French roast comfort her while he poured milk into his and slowly stirred the muddy mixture. *Why had she asked him here? What did she expect from him? Why didn't she report him to HR or have him arrested? Or both?*

"I love Jason. Very much." *Was that for Phil or herself?*

Phil sipped his coffee, staring at her over the rim, his blue eyes impaling her.

Why doesn't he say anything? "I will never leave him."

Phil set his cup down and rested his forearms on the table.

"But, our sex life leaves a bit, well more than a bit, to be desired."

He tilted his head to one side.

She put her hands flat on the table and stared at her cup. "He's impotent. Without the little blue pill, he can't sustain an erection. Truth is, he hasn't come close to satisfying me sexually for a very long time." She was blathering, but she couldn't stop herself. Before this moment, she had never confessed her frustrations to anyone. "He's six years older than me and I'm just now hitting my sexual peak. It seems I'm horny twenty-four seven, but insurance only covers ten pills a month, so we make love at best three times a week, more often than not only two."

She tried to lift her head, to look Phil in the eye, but she felt evil sharing the darkest secrets of her marriage with a man who was little better than a stranger. "I need sex more often and I like it rough. But, I can only have an affair with you," she hesitated, the word sounded so tawdry, "if you understand that discretion is paramount."

She looked up through her lashes in time to see him nod. "We can never be seen in public together except at work. No one in the world can know our relationship is anything other than professional. I'll expect you to take my secrets to your grave. And, we can only be together when we travel to the same city for work or Jason is out of town, which doesn't happen often."

He nodded again.

She hung her head, at once ashamed and excited about what she was proposing.

"You said you like it rough." His voice was husky and sexy.

Her cheeks got hot and she knew her blush probably traveled all the way down her neck.

He chuckled quietly. "You might have guessed from our first encounter that I enjoy play rape. Resistance turns me on."

Her breath came in small gasps and the tingling between her thighs became more intense.

"One of the reasons I didn't stop that night in Chicago is because your resistance contradicted how much you enjoyed what I was doing to you. Both were so incredibly hot, I didn't want to stop. And I kept thinking you didn't either."

Her chin dropped to her chest. As usual, the memories of that night taunted her with a swirling mix of emotions. She had never come so hard and so often, but she had betrayed her husband. She had begged Phil to stop, even while secretly hoping he wouldn't.

"Don't get me wrong. I'm not a dominant and I've no use for submissive women. I just like tying women up, hurting them, and forcing them to have sex with me for hours on end." He chuckled again. "I had a relationship with a sub and the sex was hot, but after a few months her submissiveness just totally turned me off."

Linda pressed her lips together, afraid to look at him. She didn't have a submissive bone in her body and would never kneel willingly before any man. But, he'd described her most intense fantasy, one she'd never thought to try in real life. Just thinking about a man physically overpowering her no matter how hard she struggled, forcing her to have sex with him, caused her breath to quicken.

"What about your girlfriend?"

Phil grimaced. "She's a survivor. Too many triggers." His fingers tipped Linda's chin up, forcing her to look into his eyes. "Do you want me to rape you again, Linda?"

A single tear crept from the corner of one eye. "Yes," she whispered.

"Can I hurt you?"

"No marks."

He rose and pulled the curtains closed over the sliding glass doors to the deck.

"Wait, what are you doing?"

He didn't answer, just lowered the blinds covering the floor-to-ceiling window in the wall next to the slider.

She stood up and cleared her throat. "We haven't yet reached an agreement on the parameters of our relationship."

"Yes we have." He stepped behind her and kissed her on the neck. "You let me know when you or your husband will be going out of town. I meet you here or there. I rape you and then I disappear, leaving no trace."

Phil's arms encircled her and tightened in a vise-like grip. Linda tried to pull free, to push his arms away, to twist out of his grasp.

He laughed at the futility of her efforts and bent her over the arm of the sofa. She heard his belt slide from the loops of his jeans and then he pulled her hands behind her back and tightened the leather around her wrists.

"No. Please stop." Why had she allowed him into the apartment? Sex with him in Chicago was one thing, in the home she shared with Jason was an affront even she couldn't permit.

Phil unbuttoned and unzipped her jeans and stripped them along with her panties off her legs despite her attempt to press her thighs together and keep her clothing on.

"Stop. I've changed my mind."

He grabbed her hair, pulling her head back, and stuffed her panties into her mouth. She tried to push them out with her tongue, embarrassed by how wet they were and how musky they tasted.

With her hands behind her back, her head buried in the sofa cushions, her feet off the floor, Linda felt helpless, unable to prevent Phil from doing whatever he wanted. And, she realized, she had no real desire to stop him. She wanted the fullness his massive cock offered, a sensation she would never know with Jason.

As if reading her mind, Phil jammed himself into her from behind, pounding her against the sofa, filling her, stroking places Jason never touched. He reached around and tickled her nub with his fingers sending her over the edge, shuddering with orgasmic intensity. Only after he had made her come hard three times and exploded himself did she realize this time he had used a condom.

Still bent over the sofa, she heard him remove it. Then he lifted her off the arm, unbuttoned her shirt, and unhooked her bra, pushing both garments off her shoulders further imprisoning her arms. He leaned over and took one nipple in his mouth, grabbing it with his teeth, and gradually clamping down so hard it hurt. She dared not pull away, afraid he would bite it off. The pain traveled from her tit all the way down to her pussy and she could feel another gush of her own juices coating her thighs.

Phil tossed her back over the sofa and she heard him rustling around in the kitchen. Then she felt his warmth next to her and a slap on her ass made her jerk. Again and again he struck her rear with a wooden spoon. She tried to roll away, but he grabbed her hair and held her in place while he paddled her behind until she could feel the heat.

This time she heard the condom package ripped open and her pussy twitched in anticipation. But, another sound she couldn't identify penetrated her consciousness and cold, slick fingers slipped into her ass. She shook her head, he was too big, she could never take him that way. But the head of his cock was pressing against her anus and she had no way to escape this new onslaught. She tried to kick backwards, but only succeeded in brushing his shins with her heels.

Slowly, he shoved his huge cock into her ass. She gasped for breath, felt like she needed to shit and that he was tearing her in two at the same time. He shoved something hard and plastic into her pussy and moved in and out of her ass. Linda growled and came hard. With one hand he pulled the plastic thing out of her then shoved it back in. With the other, he pinched one nipple harder and harder.

Again she came, her juices gushing all over his hand, her entire body shaking so violently that if she wasn't impaled by his cock she would have fallen onto the floor. By the time he spasmed inside her ass, she ached everywhere: her belly where it rested on the sofa arm, her rectum from the monstrosity thrusting in and out of it, both her nipples, her ass cheeks, and her pussy from coming around a hard piece of plastic.

Phil withdrew and eased the plastic out of her pussy. He lifted her off the sofa and held her in his arms, stroking her hair. Still panting, she pressed her cheek against the bristly hairs of his chest. Before she could completely catch her breath, he slid his hand into her hair, grabbed a fistful, and pulled her down to her knees. She tried to turn her head away, but with his other hand he forced her jaw open, extracted her panties, and shoved his semi-limp cock, coated in semen, into her mouth.

Within minutes he was hard again, pumping in and out of her mouth until her jaw ached. How could he get it up so often? And how could getting fucked in the mouth turn her on so? She hoped he wouldn't come in her mouth, only because she needed him so badly in her pussy. But, he drove himself into her again and again until he grunted and spurted his load.

"Swallow it, bitch."

Like she had a choice. Hot liquid filled her mouth and if she didn't swallow, she would spill evidence of her infidelity all over the living room carpet.

Phil left her there, on her knees, and returned minutes later with a towel from the bathroom. He covered the sofa cushions, pulled her up from the floor, and sat down with her on his lap. He held her against his chest and she could feel the quiet thumping of his heart, the breath entering and leaving his lungs. Her own breath had a raspy quality to it until they'd sat together long enough for her pulse to return to normal. The spasms in her cunt gradually subsided as her stickiness dripped out to cover his thighs.

"You're the best." Phil's hot breath tickled her ear.

She couldn't have pushed sound from her lips even if she had been able to form coherent thoughts.

He stroked her arm with one hand and ran a finger of the other up and down her thigh. She desperately wanted a nap, wanted to fall asleep in his arms. But, she could never permit him to sleep in the bed she normally shared with Jason.

CHAPTER SIX

"I'm starved. Is there somewhere we can order delivery?"

Jason had left her enough food to last the weekend. But, she was reluctant to share Jason's culinary indulgences, created with love to tempt and pamper her.

"It's not like Chicago. We don't have many restaurants that deliver themselves, but there's a service. Chinese, pizza, sandwiches, or sushi?"

"Chinese works."

She struggled to her feet and retrieved her phone, pulling up the menu as she returned to the sofa. Although she aimed for the towel next to Phil, he grabbed her and pulled her back into his lap. She showed him her phone and he scrolled down with one hand, the other caressing her thigh.

"How about BBQ Pork, honey walnut prawns, mushroom beef, and lemon chicken?"

She shrugged. It was hard to think about food while his hand wandered up from her waist and clasped her tit, pinching her nipple. Usually she let Jason order, anyway. He always picked out dishes she enjoyed, flavors that seduced her senses.

Phil offered her the phone. When she didn't take it, he asked: "Should I order?"

She nodded, her breath coming in ragged gasps as his fingers tightened their grip on her nipple. She could feel his cock hardening beneath her thighs.

After he placed the order, reciting his credit card number without retrieving his billfold, he set the phone down on the end table. "Estimated delivery time forty-five minutes." He licked the hollow of her throat. "Guess we'll have to entertain ourselves in the meantime." He slid out from underneath her, turning her at the same time so her back was against the cool leather of the sofa. Producing a condom from somewhere, he slipped it on then plowed into her sending her off again into more paroxysms of pleasure. He braced her thighs against his waist, with her ass at the edge of the cushion, his hips surging back and forth as he slammed into her over and over again. Her tits and belly jiggled from the force of his thrusts, her clit throbbed, and her pussy clenched around his cock as he drove her into one long, intense, shuddering orgasm that lasted until he groaned and came again. She had never known a man his age who could get it up as often and stay hard as long.

The doorbell rang and he swung her legs onto the sofa so she was hidden by its arm from the front entry. She heard the door open, Phil mutter thanks, and then the door close and the deadbolt turn. Phil, still naked, set the bags on the counter and opened three cabinets before he found plates. Linda managed to pushed herself into a sitting position, wrapped the towel around herself, and folded it over her breasts so it would stay on. She went into the bathroom and when she finished retrieved another towel for Phil to sit on.

She returned to find Phil had filled plates full of food, setting them on the raised granite counter of the breakfast bar that extended into the living room, along with bottles of water for both of them. After she laid the towel on one of the two bar stools, he pulled the one she was wearing off and put it on the seat of the other.

"Don't cover up such beauty."

She tried to grab the towel back, but he stood between her and the stool. "I want to admire your luscious curves every moment I'm with you."

Curves was a polite way of saying she could lose a few pounds, but the heavenly smell of garlic and honey, mushrooms and lemon made her mouth water. She clambered up onto the stool and ripped opened one of the paper packages of chopsticks that Phil had placed beside each plate.

After lunch, she closed up the containers that still had food in them and stuck them in the fridge. Phil moved the towels back to the sofa, then found an empty garbage bag under the sink and tossed in all the empty containers, the chopsticks, napkins, and a collection of used condoms. "I'll take all this with me when I leave. No trace."

The twinge of guilt disappeared the moment he grabbed her tits, pulled her against his chest, and pressed his hard-again cock into her ass. She pushed at his arm and tried to break free. He only increased the strength of his grip and twisted her around to face him. With one big hand under either ass cheek, he boosted her up onto the kitchen counter. She gasped when the cold granite pressed against her flesh, but by then his cock was inside her again.

She gripped the rounded edge, trying not to get slammed back against the raised section that made up the breakfast bar while Phil forced himself into her over and over again. He leaned forward and grabbed one nipple between his teeth, clamping down until she cried out in pain, which only made her come harder. He ground his pubes against her engorged clit while his cock stretched her open more than she had ever known.

When he finished, he pulled her against his chest, her legs still wrapped around his waist, and carried her to the sofa. Sitting with her on his lap, the tip of his cock still inside her, he pulled her face towards his. She turned away. "You're my rapist, not my lover."

A look she couldn't identify flitted across his face, but then he smiled. "I understand."

She struggled to her feet and headed to the bathroom, so sore she could barely walk. She grabbed first the sofa arm and then the wall on her way there. When she sat on the toilet, even though she needed desperately to pee, she couldn't get anything to come out for several minutes. Her thighs were sticky with her own come and her nipples hurt. On the one hand she wanted to send Phil packing, sure her body couldn't take any more abuse. On the other, she wasn't scheduled to fly to Chicago until next year and Jason wouldn't leave town without her again until Spring. After she washed up, she pulled on the bathrobe that hung on the back of the door. Keeping her foot wedged in front of it, she cracked it open and saw only an empty living room. "Phil?" No answer. "I need to call it a night. I can't... I'm so sore... please?"

Phil stepped around the corner and stood in front of the crack. "What about tomorrow?" He pushed gently at the door with one finger and she stepped aside for it to open. "I can stay over."

Linda shuffled out to the living room sofa and lay on her side. Phil lifted her shoulders and slid under her head, letting it rest in his lap while he toyed with her curls.

"I have my laptop and a change of clothes in my bag." He stroked her cheek. "I could just work for the rest of the evening and we can get a few more rounds in tomorrow morning before I leave.

Linda thought about having another man stay overnight in the condo. She decided she couldn't allow him upstairs. "If you're willing to sleep on the sofa and promise not to come up..."

"Deal." He chuckled. "Crap, I just can't get enough of you, Linda. You're just so delicious, I'd do whatever you want just for one more fuck." He kissed her forehead. "Not that I only want one more fuck from you. I want to be a part of your life, however much of your life you're willing to share with me."

She scrunched her eyes closed, unwilling to admit to him, or herself, that she felt the same way.

He traced the shape of her ear with one finger. "Anything I can do to make you more comfortable? Give you a massage? Eat your pussy?"

"The first sounds appealing, the second more than I can handle right now. My clit's sore, too."

"I promise, I'll only rub external muscles," he leaned down and whispered in her ear, his hot breath sending a chill down her spine, "this time." Phil slid out from under her and turned her onto her stomach. "Do you have any massage oil or lotion I can use?"

Linda untied the bathrobe and slipped it off her shoulders. "There should be some body lotion in the bathroom."

His legs disappeared for a moment. Then he returned and pulled her robe down, kissing her skin as he exposed it, sending renewed tension to settle between her legs. She heard the splurt of lotion and his hands rubbing together. He massaged her shoulders, reminding her of the first time. This time as the scent of vanilla almond wafted toward her nose, she was under no illusion that his massage was anything but sexual. She inhaled deeply and let Phil rub away her stress over betraying Jason.

She had to work to keep her ass from wriggling. Even though she knew her pussy was too sore to withstand another onslaught of Phil's cock, she wanted more.

He pulled the robe away, exposing her bare ass, and covering it with kisses. The pace of her breathing doubled and she could no longer keep the wriggling in check.

"Want to reconsider oral?" He dragged his tongue from the top of her ass crack, along her spine, between her shoulder blades to her neck. "I will accept the challenge of making you come without touching your nipples or clit or penetrating you." He nibbled on her ear lobe.

"You're on." Linda's voice was husky with need.

Phil kissed his way back down to her ass and licked both cheeks from one side to the other, then flipped her over onto her back. His tongue traced a wet path along the inside of one thigh to her toes. He sucked on them until she was panting. She lifted her hips up from the sofa, needing contact there despite the soreness.

Switching to her other foot, Phil sucked one toe at a time, then licked his way back towards her pussy at an agonizingly slow rate. Just as she braced herself for another onslaught on her tender flesh, he licked his way along her hip to her belly and from there to the mounds of her breasts. Linda moaned. Phil nuzzled under her left breast and slid his lips up to her areola, while his tongue darted in and out of his mouth, flicking against her heated skin. He worked his way up and down one breast and then the other, never moving past the dark brown edge of her areola.

"Please." Linda sobbed in frustration. The sound startled them both, and the realization of exactly how he could have confused her refusal with desire their first time together made her choke.

She turned on her side, coughing, trying to clear her throat. Phil lifted her to a sitting position and held her until she could breathe again. "What's wrong?"

Linda threw herself against his chest, wrapped her arms around his waist and wept. Phil ran one hand up and down her back, the other holding her firmly. "'S'okay," he whispered in her ear. "I understand."

She lifted her head and looked at him through the blur of tears. "Do you?"

"I know you're conflicted about having an affair. I see the little barriers you try to put up to delineate our relationship from the one you have with your husband. You'll let me stay here as long as I don't invade the sanctuary upstairs of the bedroom you share with him. I can rape you for hours, but we can't exchange a tender kiss."

"That first night. In Chicago." She hiccuped. "Did I broadcast my need that blatantly?"

Phil leaned back into the sofa cushions. "I'm not sure broadcast is the right word. Radiate might be more appropriate. The first time I touched you, on the shuttle, your need was palpable, which is why a handshake turned into a come on." He grinned. "Something in you resonated with me from when I watched you on the treadmill in the fitness center. Then, when we were alone in my room, it became painfully clear how much you yearned to have sex, that it wasn't just wishful thinking on my part."

She rubbed her forefingers under eyes. "You shouldn't be here. But, I'm so desperate..."

Phil put one finger over her lips. "You don't need to explain. You don't need to apologize. I will accept any role you're willing to allow me in your life with whatever restrictions you feel you need to impose." He lifted her chin with two fingers. "I do understand." He kissed her forehead, her cheeks, her nose, her chin, then stretched her back out on the sofa on her back.

She lifted her hips and he dove in, lapping at the juices that poured from her, carefully avoiding her clit. His hands stroked their way up her sides to her breasts. He gently squeezed the base of her mounds, leaving her tender nips untouched. Linda moaned and pushed into his face.

Chuckling, he pulled back enough so he could blow on her clit, sending her careening over the edge into a trembling pile of jelly.

Linda was still trying to catch her breath when she realized Phil had positioned his once-again-hard cock just in front of her lips. He didn't push in, didn't move, but stood and waited until she stuck out her tongue and lapped at his blood-engorged glans. She opened her eyes and realized he was squatting in front of her, his knees pointing outward, his quads tensed, his palms resting on the top of his thighs. She wrapped her lips around the head of his penis and sucked him inside her mouth.

His position didn't permit him to move, giving her the freedom to play with his cock, alternately bathing him with her lips and her tongue. As his breathing quickened, she teased him, pulling back, watching it bounce in the air, tickling his balls with her fingers. But, except for his breath, he didn't let on how her touch affected him.

Determined to get more of a reaction, she grabbed his cock with one hand and pulled it to her mouth. She chewed gently on the head, not as hard has he'd bitten her nipples, just enough to vary the sensation from soft flesh on flesh. He gasped and changed his position so he could hold her head and glide in and out of her mouth. Linda dropped her head on her arm and let his smooth hardness slip back and forth across her tongue. She altered from stroking him with her lips to her teeth irregularly enough so he couldn't determine any pattern to what he would feel next.

When he shot his load down her throat, she swallowed as much because she knew it pleased him as from her concern about cleaning up any evidence.

They said good night with a chaste kiss at the bottom of the stairs. Linda took a long, hot shower before she pulled on a cotton nightgown and crawled into bed. She had almost drifted off to sleep when her phone rang.

"Hi, Hon, how's it going?" She tried to keep her weariness out of her voice.

"Pretty good, actually. How would you feel about moving to Eugene?"

"I'd probably hate it. Did you get an offer from UO?"

"Practically. Enough to use to manipulate Richard. Just have to be prepared to follow through if Richard doesn't give me what I want."

"Couldn't you get an offer from a big city university? I'd rather move to Seattle or even somewhere back east."

Jason laughed. "Don't worry, babe. I don't want to leave Portland. And, I don't really want to change universities at this point in my career. I'm just hoping to use this as a negotiating tool. Worst case scenario, if Richard continues being a dick," he snickered at his own joke, "I'll check out UP and Lewis & Clark before I relocate you, promise."

Linda managed a laugh. Why had she mentioned Seattle? She would be better off spending time with Phil in Chicago than anywhere near where she lived with Jason. "You do what's best for you and I'll adapt. It's not like I have to look for another job if we move."

"Not going to worry. How are things there? Do anything interesting today?"

"I took the day off and just hung around the condo." Well, at least that wasn't a complete lie. "Did absolutely nothing useful."

"That's great. You work too much. I'm glad you took some time for yourself. Don't try to make up for it tomorrow, okay?"

"Promise."

"Love you."

"Love you, too."

Linda was surprised to see her hand was trembling when she disconnected the phone. Was it her fear of getting caught or the ease with which she lied to her husband that made her so nervous.

CHAPTER SEVEN

As much as she hated traveling, Linda found the prospect of not seeing Phil until her next scheduled trip unbearable. When she got approval for the new social media specialist on November 1, she lined up three days of interviews in Chicago for promising candidates. No one on her team commented on the irony of interviewing candidates in person for a job managing online interactions.

She checked into the hotel when she arrived just after seven in the evening and debated whether dinner or a dunk in the hot tub would improve her disposition more. The e-mail address she set up to communicate with Phil had no messages — she'd looked at it the moment she'd stepped off the plane and again while she waited in line at the hotel front desk. He hadn't written since she'd sent him her itinerary last Friday.

As she picked up the phone to call room service, she heard a tapping at the door that connected her room with the one adjacent. She frowned. *How odd.* Had someone mixed up a reservation and put her in the wrong room? The tapping became louder and more persistent. She decided to let the occupant next door know that whoever they expected to find in this room wasn't here.

The moment she turned the deadbolt knob, the door pushed open so violently she was almost knocked off her feet. Muscular arms wrapped themselves around her and a huge hand covered her mouth, preventing her from screaming. The smell of mint mouthwash and Old Spice shaving cream penetrated her nostrils and she smiled, pushing at the arms, trying to squirm free of his grasp.

Phil pulled her into the next room and tossed her on the bed. She pressed her hands against the mattress and tried to push herself off. He landed on top of her and used his weight to prevent her from escaping. Unzipping her jeans, he pulled them off her legs, stuffed her underpants in her mouth, and rolled her over and over, removing her shirt and bra.

Straddling her waist, his hard cock pressed between her breasts, he pulled her arm to one corner of the bed and fastened a leather cuff about her wrist. She tried to jerk free and discovered it was now attached by a chain to the one of the metal feet that raised the bed off the floor. By the time she realized what he was up to, Phil had her spread eagled, her wrists and ankles cuffed and chained. She was dripping juices onto her thighs and down her ass.

He jammed himself into her, grinding his public bone into her clit, slamming her cervix with the head of his cock, stretching her wide, pounding her G-spot. She exploded and the orgasm shuddered through her in waves until he grunted and filled her with his spunk.

Kneeling between her legs, still impaling her, he stared and licked his lips. "You're just so delicious. I want to rape you all night."

Linda tried to spit out her panties. Phil extracted them slowly.

"Good to see you, too." She looked at the still open adjoining door. "How'd you know I was staying in the next room?"

He laughed and pinched her nipple. "I put you there. I hacked into the hotel reservation system and made sure we were in adjoining rooms. Much more discreet than bribing someone at the front desk." He winked.

"Now, can I rape you again or do I need to feed you first?"

Linda wasn't as hungry for food as for the man leaning over her. She turned her head so she could see the clock. Only six, Portland time. "I think I can manage once more before I starve to death."

He unhooked first one ankle cuff and then the other, attaching them to her wrist cuffs. The position compressed her stomach and made it difficult to inhale. She had to take slow, shallow breaths. Intent on getting air in and out of her lungs, she hadn't paid attention to what Phil was doing until a leather paddle slapped her across her ass. She gasped. "Ouch."

"You like?" He hit her again.

Linda shook her head, but she had to admit the heat where the paddle made contact with her skin had traveled to her clit.

Phil slapped her again. "What me to stop?"

"No," she whispered.

He battered her rear over and over again, the leather paddle building up a warm glow. She wiggled her hips, needing him to take her, even as she wondered if getting fucked in this position would give her any chance to breathe at all. Phil flicked his wrist and the paddle made contact with her mons. She screamed in exquisite agony and came, hard. He laughed and plunged three fingers into her, pushing up against her G-spot, forcing her to come again.

He unclipped the cuffs on all but her right wrist and turned her on her side. Spooning her from behind, he slid inside. Hanging on to a tit with one hand and rubbing her clit with the other, he shoved himself in and out of her. Linda couldn't move. She just rode the orgasm.

When he finished, Phil cuddled her from behind and nuzzled her neck. "Miss me?"

Linda floated in post-orgasmic euphoria. She could only nod.

"Me too." He undid the remaining cuff. "Shall we order dinner?"

She moaned. She was hungry, but just the idea of walking back into her room to pick up the phone made her tired.

Phil picked up his own phone and ordered a steak. Then he lifted her into in his muscular arms and carried her to the desk in her room. "Tell them to leave it outside the door and I can get it for you."

After she ordered pork chops, Phil carried her back to his room and made her comfortable in his bed, propping pillows behind her back and head so she could eat. He responded to the knock on his door with instructions to leave the cart. The waiter insisted he had to sign the chit and Phil asked him to slip it under the door. Then he dashed to Linda's room. She had to cover her mouth not to laugh out loud at the high pitched voice he used to answer the knock there. He brought her the chit to sign and stuck it back under the door.

He retrieved his own dinner first, presumably checking the hall to make sure it was empty. When he settled her tray in her lap, Linda realized good sex could create a ravenous appetite. She attacked her food and was surprised by how good the old standard tasted. "I do have one question." She managed in between bites.

"Which is?"

"You used condoms in Portland, presumably to prevent any," she ate a French fry, "spillage. But here...?

Phil swallowed. "I had a vasectomy after Gina died. And, I can assure you, I'm clean. I'll give you test results if you want."

She shook her head. "I'll take your word for it. But you never asked about my status."

"To be frank, I didn't care. I wanted you so badly that first time, I think I would have," he licked his lips, making her twitch deep inside "taken you even if you were HIV-positive. And, I wasn't about to miss the opportunity to go find a condom."

She shook her head. "What about your girlfriend?"

He looked at her. "I'm guessing if you did have any STDs, you would have told me in an attempt to dissuade me from taking advantage of your need. Since you didn't bring it up, I was willing to take a chance on your being clean. I gave Carol the option of using condoms until I was sure, but she came to the same conclusion I did about your status."

Linda dropped her fork onto her plate. "You told your girlfriend about...?"

He tilted his head. "Of course. I would never have sex with another woman behind her back."

"But, if she knows about it?"

"Then I'm not cheating on her." He set down his fork and knife. "Carol knows that her history prevents her from meeting my sexual needs." Phil wiped his plate clean with the last piece of bread from his basket. "What time's your first interview?"

"Not until nine."

The glint in his eyes was enough to turn her on without any other stimulus. He cut off a bite of her meat and held it just above her lips while she nibbled at it.

"I should call Jason first, though."

Phil disappeared and returned with her cell and handed it to her. "Just call me when you're done." He went back into her room and pushed the door closed.

Jason's voice mail answered the call. He was probably talking to students. "Hi, Hon. Sorry I missed you. Just wanted to let you know I've arrived safely. I'm pretty wiped. I'm going to turn in early. Talk to you tomorrow."

She set the phone on the night table and stared at it.

"Phil?"

The door pushed open and the room lights flickered off. A hand covered her mouth. She struggled, but he held her down with his weight. Her already slickened legs slid against him, unable to stop him from positioning himself to take her again.

Afterwards, they lay entangled together in the bed, their breathing gradually slowing to normal. "Will you spend the night with me, Linda?"

Her muscles tensed. "I need to get up pretty early. Better if I'm by myself." She suspected he knew that answer wasn't completely truthful.

He kissed her on the forehead, released her from his leg and arms and rolled away.

Linda struggled to the opposite side of the king-size bed, grabbed her phone, and gathered up her clothing on her way back to her room. She turned the deadbolt so he wouldn't be tempted. Standing for a moment, she listened for the other door to close and heard nothing. Was he hoping she would change her mind? She dumped her clothing on the floor of the closet and brushed her teeth. Crawling in between cold sheets, her legs still sticky with his fluids and her own, Linda tossed and turned. She questioned her own lines in the sand. If Jason learned she'd had sex with Phil, would he really care that they hadn't kissed or slept in the same bed?

CHAPTER EIGHT

When the alarm went off in the morning, Linda felt as if she hadn't slept at all. She didn't have the energy to workout. Instead, she ordered two pots of coffee with her room service breakfast and stepped into the shower. Setting the taps as cold as she could stand helped wake her and prevented her from dwelling on the night before. Fortified with breakfast and caffeine, she felt almost human. Fortunately, Phil wasn't on the shuttle. He was probably in the fitness center. His physique didn't allow for missing workouts because of lack of sleep. But, then, he probably slept just fine — he believed he wasn't cheating.

Linda stuffed all thoughts of Phil to the back of her mind so she could concentrate on her interviews. Unfortunately, most of the candidates were better at writing resumes than understanding the impact of social media on customer service. They kept talking about branding, applications to remove followers who didn't follow back, and ways to increase page views. Not a single applicant mentioned content, interactivity, or how to monitor the streams for complaints that weren't directed at the company's page.

When she broke for lunch, she handed the resumes from her first four interviews to Tracy, the department secretary. "Please send them thanks, but no thanks letters."

"Nothing promising?"

Linda shook her head.

Tracy looked up at Linda from behind the row of frogs decorating her cubicle. "I know it's a long shot, but would you consider interviewing my nephew?"

Linda wrinkled her eyebrows.

"He's only twenty-three and he has no real work experience." Tracy lifted her fingers in air quotes. "But, I swear he's a social media wiz. He's got thousands of followers on his blog, and he mostly writes about companies not knowing how to use social media correctly. He tweets about customer service failures and I couldn't even tell you how many followers he has on that platform. Every time I've been on his page the number's higher."

Linda unscrunched her face and smiled. "Sounds like he may actually be what I'm looking for. E-mail me his URLs and handles and I'll review his stuff at lunch." Knowing she'd need a break from the intensity of back-to-back interviews, she had deliberately booked herself a free hour with no appointments. She walked over to the cafeteria. Grabbing a bowl of soup and a chicken salad sandwich, she planted herself in one of the small meeting rooms off the main dining hall with her tablet and clicked on the links Tracy sent.

When she returned to the office, she went straight to Tracy's desk. "If he wouldn't consider working for us going over to the dark side and if you can fit him into my interview schedule while I'm here, I'd like to talk to Mark."

Tracy grinned. "I'll tell him he can put his money where his mouth is and prove his theories." She tilted her head. "That's assuming you want to talk to him because you found them appealing?"

Linda nodded.

"Okay, don't let his appearance put you off. Talk to him for half an hour and you'll want to hire him, promise."

"We'll see." Linda headed into the conference room for her next interview with her expectations lowered and her hopes higher.

While she was listening to yet another business suit discussing metrics without understanding the connection between the numbers and the people who bought their products, Linda noted a new appointment had appeared on her calendar. When the suit left, she texted Phil to let him know she would be delayed.

Mark was a tall, lanky youngster with a head full of curly brown hair, three facial piercings and visible tattoos on his forearms. He wore blue jeans, sneakers, and a polo shirt. Linda wished she hadn't given up an hour of her evening, an hour she could have spent with Phil, to call this rogue into the office. She should have reconsidered when Tracy warned her about his appearance. He'd never fit in.

The boy's handshake was firm. "Thanks for inviting me in to discuss whether we can collaborate on a project."

Linda raised on eyebrow. "Is that what Tracy told you?"

He laughed. "No, she said you wanted to interview me for a job, but I don't need a job. My income from subscriptions to my newsletter is probably more than you're offering. And that doesn't include money I earn from my blog and YouTube channel."

She'd seen advertisements on his blog for the newsletter about what to do if a corporation wouldn't address a customer's grievance, but had thought the fifty dollar annual fee more than anyone would pay. "YouTube?"

"Second biggest search engine after Google and one of the least understood platforms by anyone over thirty."

"So why *are* you here?"

He leaned forward on his forearms. "Because Tracy's right. Your company is a perfect candidate for proving what I've been saying about how corporations *should* be using SM, but mostly aren't, and she said you at least understand that you're not doing it right. Here's what I'm thinking." He lifted one hand and held up a thumb. "You bring me in as a consultant." He added his forefinger. "You hire or transfer one, computer literate, hopefully younger employee who I will train and manage for the length of my contract. Eventually, that person will need at least one additional staff, but by then you'll have the evidence to get the higher ups to fork over whatever you need to pay for that position."

He added another finger, but didn't stop for breath. "I use the results I get here as an example to support the step-by-step SMCS guide I plan to publish."

It took her a moment to realize he meant Social Media Customer Service. He was the first person she'd heard use the two terms as one.

"Now, if the company wants all this under an NDA, I can do that. I don't need to use the name to validate the data. However, I will require that you make yourself available for anonymous interviews to support my promotional efforts for the book."

He sat back in his chair. "Whatcha think?"

Even though he'd been the one rattling off his ideas, Linda felt a need to catch her own breath. "Exactly what would all this cost me?"

"Tell you what, if I don't have to sign an NDA, I'll do it for whatever you planned to pay for the position you advertised."

"On one condition. You only get to use the company's name if we meet my metrics for success."

"I'll need to see your numbers, but that seems reasonable. Hell, if I can't make it work for you, I'm talking out of my ass, so there won't be any book."

"Also, since you'd be a subcontractor, you'll receive no benefits. I can use that to partially fund the second position you need. Given how hard it was to persuade my boss to give me one FTE, two is going to be problematic."

He shrugged. "Sounds reasonable. Mostly I need the money because this is going to take time away from my income-producing endeavors."

"Also, it might be best if you primarily worked off site." She pointed to his lip piercings. "I'm afraid you might not fit in here."

"No problem. I doubt if the equipment and offices here would meet my standards." He extended his hand. "I assume you'll want more than a hand shake, but I'll let you draw up the papers. I would like to sit in on any interviews for the staff position."

"Hang on a minute, will you?" He nodded and Linda went out to Tracy's desk. "Unless you've someone else in your family that's a social media expert, I need you to contact everyone I've got scheduled for interviews tomorrow and Thursday and let them know the advertised position has been filled, but if they want to interview for a supporting position that will be trained to take on the management role they're welcome to keep their interview slot."

Tracy gave her a mischievous smile. "Well, there is this woman in my yoga class who might work well with Mark. I'll call the ones you've got scheduled. I'm sure at least one will back out and I'll see if she can fill that slot."

Linda grinned and returned to Mark. "Tracy will let you know the schedule once she's contacted the folks I had planned to interview tomorrow for this position."

"Why don't you let me go over the resumes. I probably can save you a bunch of time."

Why not? Linda went back out to Tracy and retrieved the pile. Mark rejected all but two.

"Okay, let these know the position's been filled." She handed Tracy the larger pile. "And see if you can fit both of these and your yoga friend in tomorrow. Also, see what it would cost to change my return ticket to Thursday." Linda was torn between her impulse to fly home to Jason and her desire to stay with Phil. "Let Mark know what the interview schedule is so he can sit in. Oh, and make me an appointment with Legal. And, I'll need to see Sylvia too. Forget about changing my reservations. Just try to fit all this in before I'm supposed to leave."

Tracy gave her an *I told you* smile and Linda smiled back. She'd have to remember to include Tracy on the bonus list if Mark proved as much of an asset as Linda hoped.

CHAPTER NINE

Two weeks later, Linda was back in Chicago getting Mark and Kristina oriented to Phil's database, CS department policies, and each other. Kristina was as restrained as Mark was flamboyant, as muted as he was outspoken. She had almost no experience, but she'd impressed Linda with a cover letter, written overnight, that made it clear she understood an SM paradigm that made customer service a priority. She'd answered all of Linda's and Mark's questions enthusiastically and intelligently.

After Linda sent Kristina and Mark home at the end of their first long day, Sylvia insisted on a dinner meeting. Linda hid her disappointment and surreptitiously texted Phil.

She didn't get back to the hotel until almost nine. Kicking off her shoes, she called Jason.

"Hey, Love, hope you haven't been working all this time?"

"Unfortunately, yes. Sylvia required that I join her for dinner."

"Did she at least take you someplace nice, so you didn't have to eat the same old same old at the hotel?"

"We drove over to Café La Cave. I had a really great filet and chocolate soufflé." Of course, Jason would worry about what she ate for dinner. "But she just plied me with food so I'd accept the bad news."

"Bad news?"

"Starting next year, I'm back to monthly trips to Chicago." Bad news for Jason, good news for Phil.

"I thought... when you got promoted... wasn't quarterly part of the deal?" His voice rose an octave and his disappointment was palpable even over the phone. "You get so worn out when you travel. It takes you at least a day to really recover, sometimes more. Now you'll lose even more..."

"We compromised by changing my schedule so I'll have every other Friday off. I'll come home on Thursdays and still have a weekend to spend with you after I've recovered."

"Assuming you take the time off and don't just work more hours."

"I won't. Remember, I asked for one FTE for the social media project and they gave me two. They want me to be more hands on with them and, for that matter, the rest of my department. Realistically, once I get Mark and Kristina up and running, my job should be easier, not harder."

Jason sighed. "I miss you."

"I miss you too." She hung her head, thinking of the man waiting for her in the next room. "Do you want me to look for a job in Portland?"

"Like you'd pass up the opportunity to let Mark prove your theories about, what does he call it, SCSM?"

"SMCS." She laughed. "She did agree to let me make shorter trips. Max three days instead of four or five."

"That's good." His voice brightened. "Maybe you won't come home as wrung out as if you'd gone through one of those old fashioned washing machines."

She laughed again. "Hopefully. But, right now I *am* wrung out and I have to meet Mark and Kristina early." She hated the lie, but Phil had expected her two hours ago and her pussy twitched just contemplating what he might have planned for her.

"Get some sleep, Sweetie. Love you."

"Love you too. Miss you." At least she didn't have to fake it when it came to telling Jason how much she cared about him. If he were younger and had a libido even close to hers...

Linda sighed and pushed herself out of the chair. She *was* exhausted. Maybe she should tell Phil she'd rather wait until tomorrow. Standing in front of the connecting door, she debated with herself for only a few seconds. *Horny overrules tired every time.* She turned the latch and opened the door just far enough to give the one behind it a push. It swung into the adjacent room and she headed back to the desk. Before she got halfway there, she was struggling to break free of an iron grip around her waist, pushing at the arm attached to the hand covering her mouth.

Adrenaline kicked in as she squirmed and she almost broke free. Phil threw her face down on the bed and sat on her ass, while he pulled her blouse over her head and unfastened her bra. When he'd removed both and tossed them aside, he pulled first one wrist and then the other to the small of her back. She was already soaking wet, but the feel of scratchy hemp rope against her skin made her gush.

After he bound her wrists, Phil tied a blindfold over her eyes. Then he unzipped her skirt and pulled it off her with her panty hose and underwear. He lifted her up, threw her over his shoulder, and carried her into his room. "Brought you a present, boss."

Linda froze. She tried to slide down Phil's back, but he had a firm grip around her waist. "Let me go, I never agreed to getting involved with anyone else."

"Shut up bitch." Phil dumped her on the bed so she landed on her side and spanked her ass with his bare hand. "Boss asked for a dame and I brought him a dame. You got nothing to say about it."

She rolled over onto her back, hoping to find the edge of the bed, but someone grabbed her ankles and turned her over onto her stomach. Pillows were pulled under her hips, raising them in the air. Hands shoved her ass cheeks apart and a finger pried into her moistness. She heard the slurp of fingers pulling from a mouth.

"Yum." The voice seemed deeper than Phil's. It came from a little to her left. "Good work."

She fell on her side and kicked out, but her ankles were captured in two big strong hands. "I like em' feisty," the deeper voice said. Someone slapped her ass again and a finger probed her slippery pussy. "Wet and feisty."

A sheathed shaft plunged into her and Linda panicked. "STOP!" Her scream turned to a gurgle when another cock jammed into her mouth. She had to fight not to choke. She trusted Phil. How could he betray her like this? He moved in and out of her mouth, the man behind her staying still, with her impaled on his cock. Then Phil stopped, his cock filling her mouth, and the man behind her moved in and out.

Slowly, Linda realized there was no man behind her. Phil was leaning over, shoving a condom-covered dildo in and out of her sopping pussy. Part of her wanted to bite down on his cock, and part of her wished there were two men fucking her. She set her dilemma aside for pondering some other time, as the tension in her clit built to a hard climax. When she stopped shuddering, Phil left the dildo in place and slammed in and out of her mouth until he could fill it with his spunk. When he pulled his pubes away from her face, she fell over on her side. He pushed the pillows out of the way and lay down beside her, pulling away her blindfold.

"Had you going there for a while."

"You scared the shit out of me."

He chuckled. "Not enough to stop you from coming."

"That was *after* I figured out what you were doing."

He pulled her into his arms. "I thought you knew by now that I would never do anything to hurt you. But, tell me, if we could find the right man wouldn't you like to be fucked by both of us at once?"

A vision of Jason in her mouth while Phil slammed into her from behind sent a shiver down Linda's spine. "There is no right man. Bad enough I'm betraying my husband with one man, two would be just obscene."

"Have you thought about broaching the concept of poly? The only reason you're betraying your husband is because you don't have an open relationship. Which do you really think would hurt him more, finding out you've been sneaking around behind his back or having him know who you're with and when?"

"Don't be absurd. I'm not a swinger."

"I'm not either, but I am poly."

She scrunched up her face. "You're a polygamist?"

"Polyamorist."

"What's that?"

"Poly is Greek for many or several; amory is Latin for love. In English, it's accepting that people might want or need to have more than one intimate relationship at a time."

"You're kidding. Who the hell does that?"

"You'd be surprised how many people. My wife and I, for two. My girlfriend for three."

Linda lifted her head and stared at him.

"Gina was bisexual. She and her lover were together almost as long as she and I were. She didn't think it fair that I only had one person to love, so she insisted I have a girlfriend, too. Sometimes, when I was between lovers, she would bring home women she thought I'd find attractive. We even had several threesomes with my girlfriends over the years and once a foursome." He grimaced. "Although that didn't go over well because her girlfriend was definitely a Lesbian and having a naked male in the bed squicked her out.

"My current girlfriend, Carol, is one of the women Gina introduced me to. Carol understands my sexual needs include activities that would cause her emotional trauma and she doesn't want to deprive me anymore than I want to trigger her."

"I'm straight."

"I know. That's why I suggested a threesome with you and two men. Jason would be perfect of course, if you think there's any possibility he might be open to the idea."

Linda shuddered at his acknowledgment of her earlier thought, even though she'd not said anything aloud. "He's straight, too."

"So am I. But, we'd both be pleasuring," he lowered his voice and pinched her nipple, "or more likely raping, you. As long as he's not a complete homophobe."

Linda let her head drop down to Phil's chest, the pain in her nipple resonating through her body. She shook her head. "He'd never go for it. Old fashioned kind of guy."

"Surely, he knows that he's not keeping you satisfied sexually?"

"We don't discuss it."

Phil's mouth drooped. "That's sad. You're at your sexual peak. He shouldn't ignore your needs."

Linda scrunched her eyes, not wanting to break into tears.

Phil sighed. "Poly isn't for everyone. I don't like cheating, but I'm not willing to give you up. I guess we keep Jason in the dark, if you don't think he can handle it. I understand that you don't want to do anything that would put your marriage in jeopardy."

Linda shook her head. But at the same time, she thought about how much easier life would be if Jason could accept her affair with Phil.

As if he could read her thoughts, Phil said, "Think very carefully whether or not you should let Jason know about me. If you tell him, and he reacts badly..." Phil ran one finger along her cheek. "You don't want him to leave you."

He tilted her chin up, forcing her to look into his eyes. "Even if you think there's a possibility of him accepting poly, it's best to move very slowly. You need to see how he reacts to the concept. Maybe get caught reading a book about it. I've known women who found creative ways to bring the topic up for discussion without revealing their involvement with me."

"You're in the habit of seducing married women?"

He laughed. "No. But since I had a wife, I found it best to get involved with women who wouldn't expect me to become their primary." He shrugged. "If you decide to do anything, planning is key. Otherwise you're likely to blurt everything out all at once when your guilt overwhelms you. Remember, you can always bounce strategy ideas off me before you take any risks."

She sighed and shook her head. "Wishful thinking, I'm afraid. He'd never... he'd expect me to choose. And, I love him too much to hurt him."

Phil ran his fingers through her curls. "Okay then, enough about Jason." He grabbed her hair and yanked her head back. He plundered her mouth with his tongue and nibbled on her lip. His fingers tightened his grip on her nipple and she squirmed, trying to get away from the pain. But, her hands were still tied behind her back. The rope wasn't tight. She probably could have wiggled free if she wanted to. Only, she didn't want to.

He lowered his mouth to her free tit and grabbed her nipple between his teeth, biting harder and harder until she cried out. Shifting his body, he wormed his way between her legs and found his way inside of her. She lay on her side, one leg flung over his hip, her hands behind her back, unable to move as he slammed into her over and over and over again. Her nipples were still clamped in his mouth and fingers, but her cry of pain turned to a muted shriek of pleasure.

CHAPTER TEN

When she returned to Chicago almost two months later, Linda had tried several times, unsuccessfully, to think of a way to bring up the subject of poly during a conversation with Jason. The fear that he would leave her or throw her out, the thought of how she would react if she found out Jason had a mistress, stopped her.

He never initiated sex and lately when he turned her down three times out of five, it was hard to beg for him to make love to her. They hadn't even finished his last bottle of pills. If his disinterest was because he'd found someone else... but, she couldn't imagine him involved with another woman. Of course, he probably thought the same of her. Or maybe he suspected she was unfaithful. That could explain his recent reticence.

The distraction of holiday parties and celebrations had helped her disregard the intensity of her need. But, she longed for Phil — the press of his hard muscles against her flesh, his immense cock filling her completely, the pain that inflamed her orgasms. Normally, she hated traveling to Chicago in winter, trading Oregon's rain for the snow and bitter cold. But she had booked this trip as soon as things started returning to normal after New Year's.

To maximize her time in Chicago, Linda had arrived early and taken a taxi straight to the office. She managed to squeeze in two meetings before she caught the shuttle back to the hotel.

Linda checked in, so preoccupied that the clerk had to hand her back her own credit card. She pulled her suitcase down the hall, her laptop over her shoulder, wishing she could talk to someone about Phil. But Jason knew all her girlfriends; in fact most of their friends were couples they spent time with together.

She pushed open the door to her and pulled her case inside, setting the laptop on the desk and putting the suitcase up on the luggage rack. She flipped open the deadbolt of the connecting room door automatically, but considered telling Phil she wasn't up to sex with him tonight. She pulled off her jacket and draped it over the armchair then realized the door from the hallway hadn't closed behind her. She returned to push it shut, but it slammed open and knocked her back into the wall. A man's hand with dirty fingernails reached around the door and Linda screamed.

The door crashed closed and someone grabbed her arm, twisting it behind her back. Her shoulder felt as if was being pulled out of its socket and she thought her elbow would break. He smashed her face against the wall, her nose bending too far to one side. A hip pressed into her ass, keeping her entire body pinned to the wall. The dirty hand clamped over her mouth and the stench of stale beer and cigarettes made her choke.

A bearded mouth whispered in her ear: "Keep quiet and I won't cut you."

Linda felt hot liquid spilling down her legs and tears poured from her eyes as she realized she'd peed on herself.

"You're one hot slut, aren't you? Already so wet for me, you're creaming on my knee."

The beard was yanked away and a moment later the hand released her mouth, the hip disappeared, and the stench eased off. She turned to see Phil had her attacker by the hair and was slamming him against the door to the hall. The fury on his face scared her into the bathroom. She body slammed the door closed and pushed in the doorknob latch, while recognizing how flimsy it was.

She pulled off her wet stockings and undies, tossing them into the tub. She sat on the toilet seat, her head in her hands, sobbing until her shoulders shook. Only when she stopped to breathe did she realize someone was knocking on the bathroom door.

"Linda, it's Phil Walker from Data Architecture. The cops are here. Can you come out?"

She took deep breaths, trying to calm herself and ended up with the hiccoughs. She looked in the mirror. Her eyes were puffy, but there were no marks on her face. She shook her arm. *Not broken or dislocated.* Keeping her foot in front of the door, Linda cracked it enough to peer into her room.

A badge appeared in her line of site. "Ma'am, I'm Officer Taylor with the Schiller Park Police Department," a gruff voice said. "The gentleman in the room next door reported an assault. Have you been hurt? Can you come out and tell me what happened?"

Linda grabbed a handful of tissues from the dispenser protruding from the side of the sink vanity and pulled open the door. The bearded man was face down on the floor, his hands cuffed behind his back, blood oozing out of his nose and a bruise forming around his eye. Phil stood at the man's head, keeping a wary eye on him while watching her emerge. His face was ashen and there was blood on his blue sports shirt.

The third man, who had a stocky neck and rugged face with close cropped dark hair and a thick mustache, wore a dark blue shirt with a star badge over one pocket and a metal nameplate over the other. He had on a matching dark bomber jacket with an American flag on one sleeve and a belt weighed down with Taser, gun, radio, and various snapped and zippered leather pouches.

"Ma'am, are you hurt? Do you need a doctor or an ambulance?"

Linda shook her head and pointed to Phil. "He stopped," she looked down at the floor and pointed, "that before he... before he..." She started sobbing again.

Phil put one hand on each of her biceps, guided her over to the chair, and eased her down into it.

The officer stayed next to the bearded man. "You two know each other?"

Phil answered. "We both work for the same company and we're collaborating on a database project."

Linda nodded. She wrapped her arms across her chest and grabbed her upper arms. She was shaking. Phil reached over and nudged the room temperature up to seventy five.

"Ma'am, can you tell me what happened?"

Linda swallowed, her mouth was so dry. Phil cracked one of the complimentary bottles of water on the desk and handed it to her. She took a long swallow and then looked up at the police officer. "I checked in. I was organizing tomorrow's schedule in my head so I wasn't paying much attention to who was in the lobby." The man had to have followed her to her room, had to have known she was staying alone. She wondered if he'd heard her room number when the clerk told it to her. "I had just put my suitcase on the luggage rack when I realized the door hadn't closed behind me. I tried to push it closed," she sniveled and pointed to the bearded man, "but he slammed it into me, knocking me into the wall."

She closed her eyes, not wanting to remember, not able to forget. "He twisted my arm up behind my back, pushed my face against the wall, jammed his hip against my backside, and put his hand over my mouth. He said he'd cut me if I made any noise."

The officer scribbled in a pocket-size notebook. "Did you see a knife or any other type of blade?"

Linda shook her head. "He had me pinned up against the wall. I couldn't move, couldn't breathe."

"But, this gentleman heard you scream?"

"That was before. When he first pushed into the room. Just before he grabbed me."

"But, you're not hurt?"

"I'm hurt." Linda was angry now. "My shoulder feels like it's been dislocated. My wrist is numb. My face feels bruised, even though it doesn't look it." She spit the words out.

"I understand, Ma'am. But, at the moment all I can charge this man with is simple assault. There's no damage to the door, and you don't have any injuries requiring medical attention."

Phil took two steps toward the cop. "Excuse me, but he forced his way into this room and battered this woman. I think you need to be more ambitious in your charges."

"Did you witness any of that, sir?"

Phil shook his head.

The cop pointed his notebook at the man on the floor. "He claims the lady invited him in and they were talking when you busted in and attacked him without provocation."

Phil crossed his arms over his chest. "Then why did she scream?"

They both looked at Linda. "I want to press charges against that man for breaking, entering, assault, battery, and attempted rape. If you won't arrest him, I'll call the State Police."

"You'll have to come down to the Village Hall tomorrow and fill out the paperwork."

Linda grabbed a piece of stationary and a pen from the desk drawer. "Your name?"

"Officer Taylor, Ma'am."

"Your full name and badge number?"

"Lawrence G. Taylor. We're a small department, we don't have badge numbers."

Linda looked up from the paper. "As long as the mayor and chief of police will know who I mean when I tell them Officer Lawrence G. Taylor." She pointed at the paper.

"Yes, Ma'am." He helped the bearded man to his feet and turned him toward the door.

"Does he have identification?" Phil took another step toward the officer who put his hand on the handle of his gun.

"According to his driver's license his name is George Thomas of Lisle."

"Could we see his identification before you leave" Phil held out his hand.

"Gonna all be on the police report which you can get tomorrow." The officer extracted a license from his shirt pocket. "But, I wouldn't want you to tell the Chief I withheld information you're entitled to." He dropped it onto Phil's palm.

Phil handed the license to Linda and she wrote down every piece of information listed, then handed it back.

The cop reached into his other pocket, extracted a business card, and held it out. "Here's my contact information. You can call me tomorrow and I'll give you a police report number."

Phil handed the card to Linda. After the officer led George Thomas out of the room, Phil stood in the doorway until the elevator pinged. Then he closed the door and threw the bolt. He returned to Linda and gathered her into his arms. She sobbed onto his chest, shaking in terror, until his shirt was wet. When she tried to stop, she choked on her tears.

"Don't fight it babe. Just let it out, let it all out. You're safe now. I have you. You can let go." Phil rubbed her back and held her snug. When she finally stopped shaking, he pulled a handkerchief out of his pocket and offered it to her. Just wiping away the snot already on her face left it pretty disgusting. She sniveled.

"Have you eaten?"

She shook her head. "Not hungry."

"How about a bath? A massage?"

"I need a shower. And, I guess I should call Jason."

"I'll talk to him, if you want. He doesn't have to know anything except that I'm the co-worker who heard you scream."

She hiccoughed. "I'm not even sure I should tell him. What's he going to do about it, fly out here? He has class tomorrow."

"Would you really not let him come be with you if he wants to do that?

Linda realized she was letting Phil take on the role of comforter, the role Jason would expect to fill. How would he react if she told him about the attack, but didn't need him to console her? "No, I think it's best not to tell him. I'll send him a text after I take a shower."

Phil stared at her for a long moment. "I'm not going to tell you how to communicate with your husband. But, I can say that if this happened to my wife, I would want to know. I would take the next plane to be with her, and I would be hurt if that wasn't her expectation."

Linda hung her head.

"How do you expect to keep him from knowing what happened when this goes to court?" Phil sucked in his breath. "You don't want to tell him because of me?"

She nodded.

"Linda, I love you, but I don't want to come between you and your husband." He lifted her to her feet and stood up. "I'm leaving both doors wide open. I won't come back in here unless you want me, but I want to be able to hear you and respond quickly if you call for me. Of course, you can come to my room anytime, if you wish."

She threw her arms around his waist and held onto him until she gained enough composure to make it to the bathroom. Phil checked the locks on the door to the hallway before retreating to his own room.

After rinsing her stockings and underwear out in the sink, she wrung them out and stuck them in the laundry bag hanging in the closet. At first she just stood in the shower, letting the hot water cascade over her head and shoulders. Then, after she washed her hair, she soaped up a washcloth and scrubbed every inch of her skin until it was red. When she finally felt clean, she dried off and wrapped a towel around herself, folding it over on top. She grabbed her cell phone, pulled back the covers, and sat on the edge of the bed.

She sent Jason a cryptic text: "Had to work late. Crawling into bed now. Talk tomorrow."

Setting the alarm with time to work out, shower, and eat before her first meeting, Linda flicked off the bedside light, leaving on the lamp beside the desk and the wall light next to the bathroom. She curled up in a fetal position and pulled the covers over her head. Exhaustion claimed her. Although the bed's disarray in the morning indicated she had a restless night, she thankfully remembered none of it.

CHAPTER ELEVEN

Linda skipped the workout. While she toyed with her breakfast, she managed to talk to the police department without falling apart. She arranged to get a copy of the police report and promised she would come over and sign any papers necessary to press charges.

She had just finished her coffee when she heard a knock on her room door. She pushed the adjoining door closed as she passed it, and peeked through the peep hole. A man in a dark blue suit held a giant fruit basket.

"Yes?" She shouted without opening the door.

"Mrs. Aaronson? I'm the hotel manager."

She unhooked the latch and turned the deadbolt.

"I wanted to offer you this fruit basket as a small token of our regret for what happened."

She stepped aside and he put the basket on the table then turned and handed her an envelope. "I know your company pays for your stay here so comping you is meaningless. Instead, this certificate is good for a week at any Four Points hotel anywhere in the world. Please accept our abject apologies for what happened."

Linda allowed him to put the envelope in her hand and watched as he left the room. She had to sit down before her legs gave way.

Tapping on the adjoining door pushed it ajar. "You okay?" Phil peeked into the room.

Linda nodded, then shook her head.

He knelt in front of her and pulled her against his chest.

"The manager..." she pointed at the cellophane-wrapped basket with the envelope that was still in her hand.

He nodded. "Apparently the scumbag worked here. Until this morning, anyway. He's been fired."

She looked up, her eyes wide.

"Don't worry, he's still in jail. The manager went down to the jail and handed him his termination papers through the bars."

Linda rested her head on Phil's shoulder. She had no more tears. She felt so empty inside.

He wrapped his arms around her. "Maybe you shouldn't go to work today? I can explain what happened to Sylvia."

"Don't want everyone to know."

"If you're too shaky to work, everyone's going to figure out something's wrong anyway."

She tried to shake her head, but couldn't do so without removing it from Phil's chest. "Don't want to be alone."

"I'll stay with you."

"What about work?"

"Since you can't hide what happened from me, the way you're keeping it from your husband, you can't prevent me from staying with you to provide support. I only have one meeting today which I can get out of since I mostly used it as an excuse to come see you. I can work from the room."

Linda was too emotionally exhausted to argue with him. "Need to go sign papers."

"And, you don't want to do that alone?"

She shook her head.

He picked up her cell. "Sylvia's number?"

She found it in her contacts. Phil took her phone back and pushed send. "Sylvia? This is Phil Walker from Data Architecture. I worked with Linda to set up the SM tracking database." He paused. "Linda was attacked last night. Fortunately, I happened to be staying on the same floor. I heard her scream and was able to drag the guy off before she was seriously hurt, but she's still kind of shook up. We both have to go over to the local police department to sign the paperwork so she can press charges against the perp, but she asked me to let you know she doesn't think she's up to coming in to work today." He paused again. "I'll tell her." He ended the call and set her phone on the table.

"She said take however much time you need. She'll understand if you want to fly home after you fill out the paperwork and not to worry about the expense. She'll have Tracy cancel or reschedule all your meetings and your flight. Just send her an e-mail and let her know."

Linda just hung her head.

"I think you should let me take you to the police station and then the airport."

She moved her head an inch.

He handed her the phone. "Tracy?"

She found the assistant's contact information. He took the phone back and tapped at the keyboard then showed it to her. He'd typed: "Tracy, please cancel all my appointments and book me on a late afternoon or early evening flight home. Thanks, Linda." She closed her eyes and nodded. She heard Phil set her phone back on the table and opened her eyes just long enough to see he had sent the message.

Phil pulled out his own phone, swiped it a few times then spoke into his headset. "I need a rental car at the Sheraton in Schiller Park." He read a number from the screen. "Just for today." After a pause, he added. "That'll be fine. Thanks."

She sat, her hands in her lap, and watched him gather her things and stuff them in her suitcase.

"What do you want me to do with this?" He pointed to the gift basket, still wrapped in blue cellophane.

"Just leave it, I don't want it."

"At least take the chocolates, and maybe the cookies so you have something to snack on."

She pointed to her suitcase and he brought it over to her and she unzipped an empty outer pocket.

He untied the basket's bow, extracted several packages and tucked them into her suitcase. "You didn't eat much breakfast." He nodded toward the tray and the almost full plate. "How about an orange?" He offered one to her, but it had a green cast to it. She shook her head. "Some grapes?" She shrugged. He plucked one from the bunch and put it to her lips. She opened them enough for him to slide it in. She bit into it, but didn't taste anything. The sugar eased some of her shakiness, though, so she let him feed her all twenty-three grapes in the bunch.

He tucked her phone and the envelope into her laptop case. Slinging the strap over his right shoulder, he pulled out the handle of her suitcase, setting it on its wheels with his right arm. Then he took her elbow in his left hand, helped her to her feet, and guided her to the door of the room, locking the connecting door on the way. When they emerged into the hallway, he had her wait with her suitcase and disappeared into his own room momentarily.

When he returned, he whispered: "I locked the connecting door on my side, too."

He steered her first to the elevator and then to the front desk. When she didn't speak, he said: "Mrs. Aaronson would like to check out of room five oh three."

"Yes, Ma'am." The woman punched some keys on her keyboard, and retrieved a printout from under the desk, handing it to Linda. "Sorry you had to leave early. Hope we see you back here again soon."

Phil waited while she folded the paper and slipped it into the laptop bag. Then he carried her bag and pulled her suitcase toward the lobby entrance. Linda followed. Outside, a man leaned against the door of a blue Altima. When they pushed through the revolving door, he stood up. "Mr. Walker?"

Phil pulled out his wallet, showed the man his driver's license, signed some papers, and accepted the keys.

"Thank you, Sir." The man walked away with the clipboard of papers and Phil helped Linda into the passenger seat. She heard the trunk slam and Phil sat behind the wheel.

"Have you checked your e-mail?"

She extracted her phone and handed it to him. It was so easy to let him take care of the details. How would she survive if he sent her home?

Phil sat tapping away at her screen and then showed her an e-mail. He'd found Jason's information and typed a message. "Coming home early. Can you please meet my plane? UA1024 arriving 6:43. Thanks, Linda."

She took the phone back and changed "Thanks" to "Love" and hit send.

Phil put the car in gear and drove away from the hotel.

When they arrived at the Village Hall, Phil introduced himself as a witness and her as the victim. They were led into a small room and she had to repeat what happened for another police officer. They took Phil's statement and eventually presented them both with papers to sign. They were told they would be notified about a court date if Thomas didn't plead guilty. They made it back to the airport before noon.

Phil helped her print her ticket, but insisted she wait in line for an agent despite her whispered protest.

At the counter, he said: "Mrs. Aaronson has been the victim of an assault. I believe she may be shell shocked. Do you think it possible for me to help her get through security? We work together and it might be easier for her if she has a familiar face along."

"You would need escort credentials."

"That would be great, thank you."

"Does she need a wheelchair?"

"That might not be a bad idea, It's a very long walk."

Linda shook her head, but at the same time wondered how in the world she would hike the length of Concourse C and Terminal 1 to get to her plane. She sat in the chair, clutching her laptop case, while Phil pushed her through the bizarre music and lights of O'Hare's concourse tunnel. She kept her head down, trying to ignore everyone and everything around her.

When he settled her in the gate waiting area, he pulled out her phone. "Good," he said after swiping through some pages. "Jason will meet your plane. He's worried and asked you to call."

He showed her what he'd typed: "Can't talk now. I'll call you when I land. Love Linda"

She nodded, he pressed send, then slipped her phone back into her laptop case.

"You sure you wouldn't like some lunch? You can stay here and I'll go get whatever you like."

Jason wouldn't ask. He would have already found the one food in the airport that would tempt her to eat. When she shook her head, Phil rummaged in her suitcase. "How about some nuts?" Some dried fruit?" She kept shaking her head. "Chocolates? Cookies?" Nothing sounded appealing. Her stomach growled, but the thought of food nauseated her. She only wished they were in private so she could bury her face in Phil's shoulder and let him hold her. Since she couldn't do that, she sat in the wheelchair, clutching her laptop case. Her phone rang several times, but she didn't answer and Phil let it go to voice mail.

When the attendants opened the desk, Phil wheeled her over. "Mrs. Aaronson is feeling ill and asked me to find out if it would be possible for her to get upgraded to first class."

With a full-price ticket and the number of miles in her account, Linda wasn't surprised that she was offered a complimentary upgrade. Phil pushed her chair over to the gate area and waited until boarding started. The flight attendant wouldn't let Phil go any further. He put his hand on Linda's shoulder for a moment. "Do you think you could call me when you get home and let me know you're okay?"

She lifted her head.

He leaned down and whispered in her ear, "Remember, I'm the concerned colleague who stopped your attacker." He rose back up and said aloud to the gate agent. "I believe Mrs. Aaronson may be a bit fragile. Do you think it's possible to ask the flight attendants to keep an eye on her?"

A young man in an airline uniform took the handles of her chair. "Don't worry. We'll make sure she gets home safely."

"Thanks. Also, I don't believe she's had anything to eat today." Phil handed him the handle of Linda's suitcase. "Perhaps you could make sure she has some food?"

The attendant pushed her down the jetway. At the plane entrance, he locked the wheels. "Can you walk into the cabin?"

She nodded.

He flipped up the foot rests and took her laptop case. She used both hands to push herself up on to her feet and wavered for a moment. The man took her arm, led her into first class, stowed her laptop case under the seat in front of her and her suitcase in the overhead compartment.

She watched the young man speaking with a flight attendant in a slightly different uniform, both men looking in her direction, nodding. Moments later, a blanket covered her lap and a pillow let her lean her head back.

When she woke, the plane was in the air, a man typing away on a notebook sat in the aisle seat, and the attendant's hand was on her arm. "Sorry to wake you Ma'am, but I need to know if you want the fish or chicken?"

She shook her head.

"Please, Ma'am. I'm guessing you'll feel better if you eat."

"Chicken." Her voice was husky even to her own ears.

"Red or white wine with that?"

"Red, I guess."

She fell asleep again, but woke when the aroma of garlic and butter penetrated her senses and she discovered a steaming plate of chicken, green beans, carrots and gnocchi on a tray in front of her. For the first time since the night before she had an appetite and even the airline food tasted good. She ate every morsel and devoured the chocolate chip cookie dessert. When the flight attendant took her tray, she turned down a second split of wine.

You need to get your act together or you'll terrify Jason. She wondered if she should even let him pick her up at the airport. And, how much should she tell him? She'd have to return to Chicago for the trial, but she could coordinate that with work travel. She pulled the blanket up to her chin and clasped her upper arms. Maybe she would just tell him she felt too ill to work and decided to come home early — not horribly far from the truth.

When the plane landed, Linda waited until First Class cleared out before trying to get her suitcase from the overhead. The flight attendant was at her side in an instant. "You don't have to do that. We've got a chair waiting and I'll get your stuff down when we've deplaned the coach cabin.

She smiled at him. "I'm feeling better. I don't need a chair. If you could just help me get my bag down?"

He extracted her suitcase. "Are you sure? This is heavy and I know this isn't O'Hare, but you've still got a bit of a hike."

"I'm used to carrying more and I'm sure my husband will be waiting for me outside security." *No, he won't, he's waiting in the cell phone lot for you to call him.* She reconsidered for a moment, but she wasn't comfortable with helpless. It was one thing to let her husband or her lover take care of her, another to rely on the kindness of strangers.

Shouldering the laptop on one side and pulling her suitcase with the other, she worked her way into the cattle car torrent and made her way up the jetway. The laptop was too much weight on her sore shoulder, so she doubled over the strap and carried it in her hand. Pausing to get her bearings, she walked to the nearest moving sidewalk and extracted her cell phone, texting Jason as she rode to the end of the terminal.

Pulling the suitcase all the way through baggage claim hurt and she had to stop and wait for the pain to subside. She put the straps of the laptop bag over her intact shoulder and pulled her suitcase with the hand on the same side. Fortunately, when she emerged out into the drizzle, she saw Jason standing next to their green Forester. He kissed her and put her suitcase in the back. Slamming it closed, he wrapped his arms around her for a moment. But when he tried to release her, she held on, resting her cheek against his Gore-Tex jacket unable to let go, inhaling the comforting scent of coffee, books, and rain that clung to him.

Finally, the slap of leather against flesh startled her. "Move along you two, this is a pickup only zone." They jumped apart and she saw the traffic officer had his ticket book out.

"Sorry." Jason walked to the passenger door and unlocked it for her.

She climbed in and fastened her seat belt, staying silent while he maneuvered the car away from the curb lane and negotiated traffic to exit the airport and head for the freeway.

"Are you okay? I don't mind picking you up, but I was worried why you didn't take a cab or the Max."

"Sorry to worry you. I just don't feel very good. That's why I came home early."

They were silent again until he merged onto the freeway. "I'm sorry, Sweetie. Let's get you home and into bed and I'll bring you some soup."

She missed the days of bench seats when she could have scooted over and put her head on his shoulder and a hand on his thigh while he drove. "That would be lovely."

Merging onto I-84, they found westbound traffic heavy and Linda accepted Jason gripping the wheel at ten and two as a signal that he needed to concentrate on driving. She didn't want to talk, anyway. She just wanted to be home, on the sofa, in his arms, with a log burning in the fireplace.

CHAPTER TWELVE

She walked into their apartment and was inundated by the delectable scent of garlic, onions, and beef broth. *Home.*

Jason followed with her luggage. "When you said you were coming home, I figured I'd have dinner ready." He propped her suitcase up against the counter and glanced at the timer on the slow cooker. "Should be done in another hour or so." After hanging up their coats, he asked, "Are you hungry? I could fix you a snack to tide you over. I know that's kind of late for dinner."

She shook her head and dropped onto the sofa. "They took pity on me at O'Hare and upgraded me to first class. I ate on the plane." She kicked off her shoes and curled her legs up under her. "What I'd really like is a cup of tea, a fire, and a cuddle."

Jason stepped from behind the counter long enough to bow at the waist. "Your wish is my command, my dear." He filled the kettle, put it on the stove, and then knelt in front of the fireplace. By the time the kettle whistled, he had a roaring blaze going.

Mesmerized by the flickering colors as the flames consumed the logs, Linda was startled when Jason sat on the sofa next to her.

"We can get started on the cuddle while your tea is brewing." He opened his arms and she fell into them.

Instead of taking comfort, she couldn't help thinking she didn't deserve his cuddles or belong in his embrace. The kitchen timer chimed and she tried to regain her composure while he poured tea, added honey, and handed her a steaming mug. She held it to her lips, letting the steam envelop her face.

He sat down next to her and put an arm over her shoulders. "What's

71

wrong, Linda? You're distracted, your hands are trembling, and you've been crying. Did something happen at work? If you lost your job, you don't have to be afraid to tell me. We can manage. It'll be difficult, but we can get by on my salary for a while if we have to, especially if you're eligible for unemployment or severance..."

She shook her head. "I was attacked."

Jason took her cup and set it and his own on the table next to the sofa, pulled her into his arms, and rested his cheek on the top of her head. "Are you okay? Did you see a doctor? Did they catch the guy? Why didn't you call me so I could fly out and take care of you? You shouldn't have been traveling alone."

"Physically, I'll survive." If her shoulder still ached in the morning, she probably should make a doctor's appointment.

He held her tighter. "You want to talk about it?"

"Not really." She wrapped her arms around his waist. "Please just hold me."

They sat watching the fire until the slow cooker pinged.

Jason stroked her hair. "It switches to warm automatically if you're not hungry yet."

She snuggled in closer until her stomach grumbled.

"I guess that answers that question." Jason extracted himself and returned to the kitchen. She reached for her tea, but left it when she realized it was stone cold.

"I can heat that up in the microwave for you." Jason pulled down bowls and lifted the lid from the cooker to fill the condo with its tantalizing aroma. Linda added another log before she went to the bathroom to wash up. Looking at herself in the mirror she could see no evidence of what she'd endured. But, in her mind's eye the red letters of "adulterer" flashed under her reflection. Gripping the granite vanity top, she broke into tears, her shoulders shaking as she tried to keep the sound of her sobs from escaping the closed door. She wept until she heard Jason's knock.

"Are you all right in there?"

She sniveled. "Be out in a minute." She washed her face in cold water, but her eyes still looked red rimmed and puffy.

Jason was waiting for her outside the door. He took one look at her face and wrapped his arms around her again. "If you can't talk to me, maybe we should call the rape crisis hotline?"

Linda took a deep breath, trying to still her trembling. "I wasn't raped. One of my colleagues heard my screams and pulled the guy off of me before..." She pressed her lips together, not wanting to think about what would have happened if Phil hadn't barged through the adjoining door.

"I'm not sure that matters, especially given how upset you are. I'm guessing you need to talk to *someone*."

"I'll be okay." She didn't realize she was lying until after she said the words. But, she also knew it wasn't the attack that left her sobbing and trembling in her husband's arm. And, who the hell could she talk to about betraying this wonderful, sweet man? Linda's tears flowed anew, wetting Jason's shirt.

He sidestepped with her over to the sofa and sat her down. Lifting one of the bowls from the wooden tray he'd set on the coffee table, he speared a piece of beef with a fork, blew on it, and fed it to her. She sobbed, almost choking on the morsel and everything it represented.

Jason had always done the cooking — she had trouble making coffee. But, his interest in culinary arts, in tempting her with ever more complex creations and goodies from every bakery in town, increased as his libido plummeted.

He handed her a glass of ruby red wine and she took a cautious sip. When it stayed down, she reached for the bowl, but he held it out of her grasp. Bite by bite, he fed her every bit of beef, potato, onion, and turnip, pausing occasionally to chew something from his own bowl. Tears continued to leak out of Linda's eyes, but she kept the wrenching sobs at bay. She indulged in a second glass of wine, hoping it would help her sleep. Jason produced cherry tarts from Pearl Bakery for dessert and served them with her favorite French vanilla ice cream.

Linda left her suitcase and laptop unpacked and crawled into bed, slipping into a food and wine induced coma. When Jason joined her, he worked his arm under her neck and pulled her onto his shoulder. She turned over, flung her arm across his chest, and hugged him tight until sleep loosened her grip.

The next morning Jason offered to call in sick to school, but Linda couldn't allow that, not with his tenure hanging in the balance. She buried herself in work and e-mail, but avoided questions about when she would return to Chicago and reschedule her cancelled meetings..

Phil called just before noon. "How are you holding up?"

Linda burst into tears at the sound of his voice. She missed him, wished he were sitting next to her, as ready and willing as Jason to comfort her. Was it greedy to want both of them?

"I guess that answers my question. Do you want me to change my flight back tonight to Portland instead of Seattle? I can find a hotel near there and you can come over to cry on my shoulder while Jason's at school."

She shook her head, but couldn't stop crying long enough to respond.

"I'll be on the..."

"No. You don't understand." She darted into the bathroom, grabbed a box of tissues, and returned to her chair. "You're why I'm so upset." She muted the phone to blow her nose.

"You mean because I busted that guy's chops?" He sounded amused.

"You know that's not what I mean." She took a sip from her water bottle. "I feel so dirty. I'm such a slut."

"You're not a slut. You're a woman with needs, needs that can't be met by one man alone. Your problem isn't that you're having sex with another man. You're cheating on your husband because you're not telling him about our relationship. "

"As much as I care about you, Phil, I love Jason. We've been together for almost twenty years. I'd never leave him for you."

"I'm not asking you to. I'm willing to share. But, I'm guessing from what you've said that he's too straight laced to even consider the idea." When she didn't answer, he added. "You can't make a rational decision when you're traumatized and feeling guilty."

Linda sobbed. "What if he leaves me? I know he'll feel betrayed. I would."

"Then, don't tell him."

"I... won't." Linda bawled. "Gotta go." She ended the call, leaned on her desk, and buried her head in her arms. The phone rang again and Linda almost didn't look at it, figuring Phil was calling back. Then she saw Jason's picture on the screen, and answered it.

"How are you doing, Sweetie?"

She tried to steady her voice, but only a sob came out.

"You sure I shouldn't come home early? I can get my T.A. to take my last class."

"No." She muted the phone again so she could blow her nose. "You don't want to upset Richard."

"Whoa. You're more important to me than tenure. I'm leaving now."

"Please don't." She could picture him pausing with his finger on the off button of his headset.

"I'm probably better off alone, for the moment. If you come home, I'll just sit here and blubber. At least alone, I stop crying enough to work for a little bit at a time."

"You're sure?"

"I'll text you if I change my mind."

"Promise?"

"Yes."

"Okay, I'll call before my office hours start."

Linda ended the call and blew her nose, filling the wastebasket under her desk with tissues. She managed to work straight through until she got a text from Phil.

"Just checking in. Is Jason home yet?"

She glanced at the time. "Probably not for another couple of hours. I've been working."

"Feeling better."

"No."

"Let me know if you want me to come down there."

"I'll be okay."

"Well, then, let me know when you reschedule your trip to Chicago so I can join you."

"Maybe it would be better if we weren't in Chicago at the same time."

"You know you don't mean that."

He was right, but she didn't have to admit it. No amount of guilt and shame could change how Phil made her feel. She didn't answer him and erased the entire conversation from her phone as well as the record of his earlier call.

CHAPTER THIRTEEN

Jason brought home an entire French silk pie and a bottle of her favorite Zinfandel. He set both of them, together with the mail, on the counter. The white plastic envelope from the pharmacy sat conspicuously on top of the pile. They both ignored it.

With the help of two glasses of wine, she managed to get through her bowl of pot roast without sobbing.

"Maybe you should look for a job here in Portland." Jason set a plate in front of her with a quarter of the pie.

"Whoa. I hope you're planning on sharing that with me."

"If you insist. But, you can have it all if you want."

"I can't eat my way to peace of mind."

He cut off a fork full of the chocolate confection and held it to her lips. "Why not. Always worked for my mom."

She let the combination of rich chocolate mousse, whipped cream, chocolate cookie crust, and dark chocolate shavings soothe away her guilt. He offered her another bite and she raised one eyebrow. He popped that one in his own mouth then cut off another bit for her. She closed her mouth too soon and ended up with whipped cream on her lips. Before she could lick it off, he leaned over and stroked her lip with the point of his tongue, pushing the errant morsel back into her mouth.

She reached around behind his neck and prevented him from pulling away.

When she released him, she pointed at the envelope still unopened on the counter. "I wouldn't mind breaking into that tonight."

He pulled back and looked into her eyes, worry crinkling around his own. "You sure?"

"Very." She closed her eyes, leaned forward, and met his lips with her own, opening them, welcoming his tongue into her mouth. He pushed in slowly as if not believing her and she sucked him in the rest of the way. Tenderly, he put one hand on either side of her face, caressing her cheeks and pulling her closer.

He ended the kiss by planting his lips on the tip of her nose. "Why don't I take my pill and we can finish dessert before we go upstairs."

She smiled at him. He corked the wine bottle, put the rest of the pot roast and pie in the fridge then rummaged in the junk drawer for a scissors. He extracted one of the tiny blue pills and swallowed it with the rest of the juice in his wine glass.

When he returned to the table, he sat in the chair next to hers, pulled her into his lap, unbuttoned her shirt, unhooked her bra, and pulled it below her breasts. He filled his fork with whipped cream and mousse and brought it toward her lips. With a twinkle in his eyes, he turned it over and the pie landed on her breastbone. She gasped from the cold, especially when he smeared it over her breasts with the fork.

Returning the fork to the plate, he lifted both her breasts in his hands and slowly licked all the gooey mixture from her left tit, replacing sticky sugar with his warm saliva. He planted a sloppy kiss halfway between her nipple and her chest then turned his attention to her right breast. By the time he had cleaned all the pie from that breast, they were both panting and she could feel the beginning of an erection stirring under her rear.

She rose to her feet, took the plate of pie in one hand, grasped his with her other, and led him up the stairs. Setting the plate on the night stand, she flipped back the covers, then turned and unbuttoned his shirt. He pulled it off then removed hers and tossed it with her bra in the general direction of the lounger in front of the sliding glass door. Waiting until he faced her again, she slowly]inched down the zipper of her skirt.

He reached forward and pushed it and her panties down over her hips, then dropped to his knees in front of her. Pulling her toward him with one palm on either ass cheek, he pushed his nose into her pubic hair and inhaled. Sticking out his tongue, he thrust it into her slit and found her nub. Linda fell back on the bed.

Jason pulled her slippers and pants off, then upended the pie plate on her belly.

"Hey, I wanted *some* of that."

He chuckled. "Don't worry, you'll get yours." He kicked off his loafers, stripped out of his slacks and boxers, and crawled up on the bed with her. He coated his semi-erect cock in the sticky mess on her tummy, then planted himself behind her head. Leaning over, he positioned his cock so she could take it in her mouth while he licked pie off her stomach.

Sucking him in, she swallowed a mouthful of chocolate sweetness. She held his balls in her hands and ran her tongue up and down his hardening penis, making sure to remove all traces of pie. By then Jason had cleaned off her tummy and was licking his way back to her mound, pausing to make sure he'd extracted all remains of chocolate from her bellybutton.

He was finally hard enough for her to pull him in and out of her mouth and she lifted her hips toward his lips, desperately needing him to touch her clit. He obliged, pushing into her slit and manipulating her nub with the point of his tongue. Her breath came heavier and her juices flowed. Jason lapped them up, sighing contentedly. He wrapped his lips around her button and sucked until the tension started to build.

She pushed her tongue into the slit of his cock and sucked hard on his glans. He jerked his hips back, pulling his cock out of her mouth. Lifting her head, she tried to get her lips back around it. But, Jason turned around so he was lying next to her, flat on his back. He pulled at her arms until she climbed on top of him and guided him inside her.

Reaching up, he caressed her tits with his palms, gently squeezing them. She wondered what he would do if she asked him to pinch her nipples. In all their years together, they'd never tried anything remotely kinky. Once they'd made love in a cave hidden away on a deserted island accessible only by boat. Other than that, it was in bed, face to face, usually with her on top so he could play with her tits. Even if she expressed a desire to do something out of the ordinary, he wasn't long enough to take her from behind or thick enough to stimulate her G-spot unless she straddled him.

Linda pushed her traitorous thoughts away and concentrated on contracting her pussy muscles around Jason's cock. She had a man who loved her, who was devoted to her happiness. Why couldn't she be satisfied with mediocre sex ten times a month? Until she'd met Phil, that had been enough, almost.

Jason pushed his hips up into her and kneaded her clit with his thumb while he massaged one tit with his other hand. She used her leg muscles to raise and lower herself on his cock until the intensity finally released and she shuddered, dropping down onto his chest. Holding onto her ass, he pushed himself up and dropped back down. She rubbed her clit against his pubic bone and let the tension build again. His speed increased and she wiggled to intensify the pressure, desperate to come once more before he did.

She'd read about sildenafil citrate lasting four to six hours. Wishful thinking in her case. Once Jason came, that would be it for several days, blue pill or no blue pill. Feeling guilty, she raised her head off his chest and kissed him hard. He tickled her lips with his tongue until they both exploded. When Jason softened and slipped out, Linda eased herself onto her side, keeping her head on his shoulder. He wrapped his arms around her.

The next thing she knew, moonlight spilled through the bedroom window. Jason lay flat on his back, his breathing strong and steady. Linda shivered and pulled the covers over them both. Resting on one elbow, she watched the tranquil, sleeping face of her husband. Not as ruggedly handsome as Phil, his good looks were more boyish. Wavy dark brown, almost black hair, soft cheeks, a beard that he could skip shaving all weekend and it still wouldn't grow out enough to irritate her skin. Although he walked half a mile each way to school five times a week, he was a tad pudgy around the middle and if he grabbed her, she could break free of his arms without difficulty.

Linda bolted from bed and ran into the bathroom. She sat on the toilet, sobbing at her duplicity. How could she lay naked in bed with her husband while she compared him to her adulterous lover? Jason deserved better. She couldn't continue to deceive him. But, how could she live without Phil? After making love with Jason, she was still horny and knew it would be at least several days before he would make love to her again.

Phil on the other hand, left her wrung out and satiated. He filled her in ways Jason never could, shared her darkest fantasies, and his libido exceeded her own, something she had never thought possible.

"Linda, what's wrong? Can I come in?"

"No!" She flung herself at the door, pressing her back to it, and slid down until her bare butt hit the cold tile, using her weight to keep the door closed.

"Please, Linda, let me in. I can't help you if you shut me out."

She wept, unable to speak, her tits jiggling, her hands shaking with the force of her sobs. The door pushed against her back, but she put her bare feet flat on the cold floor and held her ground.

"Please Linda. You don't have to talk if you don't want to. Just let me hold you, take care of you. I can't stand to see you suffer like this. Please."

Unable to resist the pleading in his voice, Linda fell over on her side. When she curled up in a fetal position, there was just enough room for him to push the door open and squeeze inside.

"Geez, you're going to freeze." He left and returned with the quilt from the bed. He wrapped it around her and pulled her off the floor into his arms. He sat there on the hard tile, rocking her back and forth. "There, there," he whispered. "You're safe now. No one can hurt you while I'm here."

"But, who's going to protect you from me?" She sobbed, shaking in anguish and frustration.

"What in the world do you mean, Sweetie. I love you, you love me. We'll get through this, even if we need to get you professional help. My insurance will cover counseling, if yours won't."

She couldn't stand it. He was being so nice, so good to her. She didn't deserve his kindness, his affection, his concern. She was a two-timer, a cheat, a whore. He should throw her out in the street, not sit on the cold bathroom tile holding her. Her breathing was ragged, every inch of her trembled and her sobs emerged in gulping shudders.

"Please go away." She gasped. "I don't want to hurt you any more than I already have."

"Hurt me, darling what are you talking about?" He covered her forehead and cheeks with kisses, licking away her tears. "You're the best thing that's ever happened to me. You've made me incredibly happy. You're the only woman I've ever loved and the day you agreed to be my wife was the most thrilling day of my life." He held her tighter. "You're upset by what happened. Tomorrow, I'll make some calls and we'll get you in to see a counselor..."

"I don't need a counselor. I need a scarlet letter, you should throw me out and stone me."

"What in the world in the are you talking about? First of all, you said he didn't rape you. And I know you screamed — you said a co-worker heard you."

She wept, choking on her own mucous. "You don't understand."

"I know. That's why I want to help you find a counselor. Someone who *will* understand."

Linda tried to push away, pressing her palms against Jason's chest. He just gripped her tighter. She was trembling, shaking from frustration, fear, and loathing for her despicable self. "No... No... No... No."

"I'm calling the doctor. Maybe I can get someone on call to prescribe you something."

She dropped her chin to her chest and bawled until nothing came out. Jason handed her a box of tissues and she used half of it before she could breathe through her nose. His mouth was pinched closed, his eyes crinkled with worry, his chin quivering. He had to teach two classes tomorrow. She couldn't let her guilt keep him up any longer. Jason needed sleep and so did she.

Patting his hand, she pushed herself to her feet. He watched her warily while she splashed cold water on her face and then used the toilet. "We should go back to bed," she said after washing her hands.

"You're going to be okay?" The worry lines hadn't eased and his chin still quivered.

"I don't know. I just am too tired to think about it anymore. We both need to work tomorrow."

Jason followed her into the bedroom, and covered her with the sheet when she crawled into bed. He spread the quilt across the mattress then returned to the bathroom. By the time she heard the toilet flush, she was falling asleep, emotionally and physically exhausted. She was barely aware of him returning to bed, kissing her on the forehead, and holding her hand.

CHAPTER FOURTEEN

Instead of working, Linda spent the next day contemplating different ways she might explain Phil to Jason. She thought about Phil's contention that the problem wasn't having sex with another man, it was lying about it. Maybe that was the approach she needed to take. If she assured Jason that if forced to choose, she would pick him, if he knew he came first, maybe he would open up to the idea.

She devoted an hour to critical e-mail then cleaned up and fixed dinner. They still had leftover pot roast, so Linda made a salad to go with it and set the table.

Jason looked haggard when he arrived and presented her with a bouquet of dahlias. "Are you feeling better?" He retrieved a vase from the top of the cabinet.

"A little." She tossed balsamic vinegar, olive oil, and a spice mixture into the salad, hoping he would appreciate that she didn't just pour something from a bottle onto his carefully selected lettuce. "We need to talk."

"If you wish." Jason pulled out the rest of the pot roast and distributed it between two bowls which he placed in the microwave. "I don't want you to talk if it's going to upset you again."

She set the salad on the table and sat down. "I need to tell why I'm upset." He started to speak and she raised her hand. "It's not what you think."

Jason sat down across from her and ground pepper onto his salad.

"The man who attacked me slammed the door to my room closed."

Chewing on his salad, Jason gave her a confused look.

"The man who rescued me, Phil, was able to do so because the connecting doors between our rooms were unlocked."

"That's fortunate. How did he know?"

"He knew because we always unlock them when we arrive at the hotel. We've been having an affair for almost four months now." Ironic that she automatically counted from the first time Phil had sex with her.

Jason's jaw dropped open and his fork clattered as it hit the table and bounced off.

Linda closed her eyes and hung her head so she wouldn't have to see the hurt in his eyes. "I love you Jason, I don't want to live without you. But, even with the pills you..." She took a deep breath. "I love Phil, too, but in a different way." She picked up her wine glass and drank half of it in one long swallow. "He meets my sexual needs."

"I try, damn it." Jason hit the table with his fist. "I hate the fact that I need a pill to make love to you, but I try. And you come, don't tell me you've been faking that, too?"

She shook her head. "Yes, with you I come once or twice. But with Phil, I lose track of how many times I come. And, it's much more intense. He's much bigger and I need that." She bunched up her napkin in her fist. She tried to relax and spread it across her lap.

"You're leaving me?" Linda looked up. Jason sat with his palms against the table, his back pressed into the chair, his lower lip quivering.

She shook her head. "I don't want to."

"But?"

"But, I don't want to give up Phil, either. What's tearing me apart is seeing him behind your back. I hate deceiving you."

"But, you don't hate having sex with a man who's not your husband," Jason shouted.

Linda wiped his spittle off her face and took a deep breath. "If we had an open relationship..."

"You want me to approve of your having sex with another man? I should be your willing cuckold?"

"You wouldn't be a cuckold if we had an open relationship."

He stood up and leaned over so his face was right in front of hers. "I never realized how little respect you had for me. I know my libido doesn't match yours, but I take the damn pills. I try to please you. I've devoted my life to making you happy. I learned how to cook for you. And this is the thanks I get." He sat back down, slumping in his chair.

A single tear crept down Linda's cheek. "Please," she whispered, "don't make me choose. I love both of you. You don't ever have to meet Phil, I can see him when I'm in Chicago or I can visit him in Seattle. I'd still be with you most of the time. I'm not interested in living with him."

"No, you just want to *shtup* the son of a bitch." He leaned his elbows on the table and held his head in his hands.

Linda speared lettuce leaves with her fork, brought them to her mouth, then set them back into her bowl. She reached for her wine glass and discovered it was empty.

"Sex is that important to you that you'd destroy everything we've built over twenty years together?"

"You have no idea what it's like to be horny all the time, to always be so frustrated I could scream."

He looked up at her and tilted his head to one side. "Actually, I do. That's what being a teenage male is like. But, I just wanked off a dozen or so times a day. I didn't cheat on my wife."

"You didn't have a wife. And, if you'd had the opportunity then, you would have fucked anyone who would have opened her legs for you."

He pressed his lips together and looked at the table.

"What would you think if I told you I was kinky and that I really get off on rough sex?"

He looked up at her. "I'd suggest that you probably should see a shrink."

"Why? What's wrong with kinky sex?"

"I don't... I couldn't... I'm not..."

She put her forearms on the table and leaned toward him. "Exactly. You're not kinky and I haven't asked you to try. Our relationship, our intimacy, comes from so many other things than sex. But, I am kinky. And I need so much more sex than you do. I don't want to take anything away from you. Have you noticed anything different these past few months?"

His chin crept up towards his nose. "Yes."

Linda stared at him.

"You've been..." he rubbed the back of his neck, "calmer. More centered. I thought you'd gone through the change or something."

"So, you're agreeing that not only does my having sex with Phil not take anything away from you, it makes me easier to live with."

"That's not what I said." Jason pushed back from the table, knocking his chair on its side, and stomped up the stairs.

Linda sat stunned and drained. Finally, she pushed herself up from the table and put the uneaten salad back in the fridge. She took the pot roast out of the microwave, scraped it back into the crock, and stuck that in the fridge as well. After putting the dirty bowls, tableware, and glasses in the dishwasher, she wandered over to the bottom of the stairs. She stood there unsure if she should go up or sleep on the couch. Creeping up the stairs, she peered through the railing supports. The bed hadn't been touched, the chair was empty. She found Jason standing outside on the deck, watching the river.

Coming up behind him, she slipped her arms around his waist. He put his hands on her forearms, started to push them off, then held them against himself. They stood there, her cheek pressed against his back, until she shivered. Then he did pull her arms apart and led her back inside, sliding the door closed, turning the latch, and pulling the curtains across the doorway.

He dropped into the lounger and pulled her down into his lap. "I can't decide," his voice was hoarse and she realized he'd been crying, "which would be worse. Losing you or knowing you're having sex with another man."

She started to speak, but he put his fingers across her lips. "I need to think about this. I don't want to give you up, but I don't know if I can share you, either."

"Thank you for at least considering..." Linda stayed in his arms until he gave her a gentle push. Then she went into the bathroom to get ready for bed. When she returned, Jason was gone. Halfway down the stairs, she saw he had stretched out on the sofa, wrapped in the spare quilt. Tears streaming down her face, she stumbled back up the stairs and crawled into the empty bed.

Jason was gone by the time Linda showered, dressed, and came downstairs. She fixed herself a bowl of cereal and went to work. Her phone stayed next to her keyboard, but only Phil's number came up. She ignored his calls. Jason still hadn't returned after she ate the leftover pot roast for dinner and crept into bed. Just after midnight, she woke up when the front door opened and closed and lights came on downstairs. She debated going down, but she heard running water then all the lights were extinguished, and silence settled on the condo. She cried herself to sleep.

When Linda went downstairs in the morning, Jason was still asleep. She made coffee, then pulled out the griddle and prepared French toast, his favorite and one of the few dishes she could cook without burning something. He sat up just as she flipped the first batch over. Without saying a word, he folded the quilt and went upstairs. She heard the shower running a few minutes later. Stacking the toast on a plate, she stuck it in the oven and turned it on warm. Hoping, she set the table for two and sat in the seat facing the stairs while she sipped her coffee.

When Jason came down, his hair was still wet and he wore clean jeans and an OPB tee shirt. He opened the closet and reached for his jacket.

"I made French toast."

He hesitated.

"I think we still have some Dundee marmalade."

He closed the closet. Linda poured coffee in the second mug and added milk and sugar. Then she got up and retrieved the plate from the oven and the white marmalade crock from the fridge. Jason sat down at the table and let her pile French toast on his plate.

Slathering marmalade on each piece, he ate mechanically without looking at her or saying a word. He devoured five pieces. She wondered how long it had been since he'd eaten, but didn't dare ask.

"I can make some more."

He emptied his coffee cup. "That's okay, thanks." He picked up their plates, carried them around the counter into the kitchen, and put them in the dishwasher. She sat with her back to the kitchen, listening to him fill and start the dishwasher and wash the griddle. She hung her head. The noise in the kitchen came to a halt and Jason stood in front of her. She looked up to see his eyes were as red as hers. Jumping up, she grabbed him around the waist before he could slip away again. At first, he just stood there. Then, finally, slowly, his arms slid across her shoulders and held her.

Her tears wet his shirt. "I love you." Jason didn't respond and she wept harder. "What are we going to do?"

"Get a divorce, I guess." He pushed her away and moved into the living room, sinking down onto the recliner.

"Why?"

"That's a stupid question. You're in love with another man." He sat with his fists on the arms, his feet flat on the floor.

She shook her head. "I'm in love with you. I never stopped loving you."

"And, if I ask you to choose him or me?"

Linda dropped to her knees in front of Jason and rested her cheek on his thigh. "Please don't make me choose. I need you both. In different ways. For different reasons. But, I'm not sure I could live without either of you."

"You're telling me that if I left you, you wouldn't be running off to move in with this guy the next day?"

"I have no idea if I could live with him, and to be honest I have no desire to. Besides, he has a girlfriend."

"Geez So, he's a two-timer, too?"

"No, his girlfriend knows about me." She lifted her head and looked at

Jason. His face looked worn and drawn. He seemed to have aged a decade overnight. "You're the man I always want to live with, share my days with."

"Humph. Days. But you want to spend your nights with him?"

"I want to be able to have sex with him once or twice a month."

"And, he's okay with this? His girlfriend is okay with this?"

"She doesn't meet his sexual needs either. And, he's willing to share me with you. He's the one who suggested I tell you about him weeks ago." Well, that wasn't completely accurate. Once she explained how fusty Jason was, Phil had warned her that telling him might not be the best choice. "He doesn't like hiding our relationship from you."

"But, he's okay fucking another man's wife? And I've been your husband for nineteen years. I'm sharing you with him, not the other way around."

"Neither one of you owns me. Neither one of you can meet all my needs." He winced.

"Do you really think we should divorce just because you're impotent?"

His voice dropped so low she could barely make out his words. "I've done everything I can to try to make you happy."

"And, in every way but one you do. Emotionally, you're my perfect husband and partner. But, physically... I'm still young, I've just hit my sexual peak. I don't want to give up a fulfilling sex life and I shouldn't have to at my age. No amount of comfort foods and treats can replace sex."

"So, you want a divorce?" Every muscle in his face sagged.

"No." She dropped her head back down to his lap. "I want to be married to you. I just don't want to be horny all the time, never getting enough sex, never..." She looked up, trying to see beyond the hurt in his eyes to the love for her she hoped was still there. "Look, before I met Phil, I was resigned to not getting enough sex. But, I was never happy. You sensed that. And I seriously doubt I could be happy if he were the only man in my life."

He sighed. "I don't think I can do this. Every time you fly off to Chicago, I'll be haunted by visions of you and this Phil guy banging each other all night. I mean, do you even work while you're there?"

"Do you really think the company would pay me to fly to Chicago and not show up at the office every day?"

"How would I know? You manage all the finances. You could be paying your own way to Chicago and I wouldn't have a clue."

Linda hung her head. She couldn't blame him for not trusting her under the circumstances. She bit her lip, but still tears spilled out again.

He slid to one side so he could rise to his feet. "You can have the condo. Hell, I don't think I could live with the memories."

She pushed herself up from the floor and stood in front of him. "I don't want the damn condo. I want you."

Jason stared at her for a very long moment, stepped around her, pulled his jacket out of the closet, and slammed the front door behind himself.

Linda fell onto the sofa, sobbing. She supposed she should call Phil, let him know what had happened. But he'd probably just say "I told you so." All she really wanted to do was crawl into a deep dark hole and hide from both of them.

CHAPTER FIFTEEN

By the time Jason had walked across the Burnside Bridge, the rain had soaked his clothing. He trudged south on Martin Luther King Drive, head bent under his hood, oblivious to the city around him, and crossed back over the Morrison. He debated continuing south and across the Hawthorne, but it was dusk already and he was cold.

He ducked into a coffee shop and nursed an extra large until full dark descended and the clerks upended the chairs on the table, swept the floors, and turned off the lights. Shuddering under the awning, he looked up and down Southwest Second Street trying to determine where he should go next. He couldn't think, he couldn't even decide if he was hungry or not. *How will I survive without Linda?* The wail reverberated through his consciousness blocking out any other thoughts, hampering his awareness of the cold, his wet jeans, his soaked sneakers.

He found himself standing outside their building staring up at the lights in the windows of their condo, unaware of how he'd arrived there. Huddling under the bus shelter, he watched until all the lights blinked off one by one. He checked his phone. After midnight. Linda was almost always in bed by eleven. Was she alone, or had she called her paramour to come rushing into her arms.

Without looking, almost hoping a car wouldn't see him in his dark jacket, he walked across the street halfway between two intersections. Unfortunately, only one car sped by and two lanes separated them.

Standing outside their doorway, his jacket dripping puddles at his feet, he fumbled for his keys then stared at them, his hand shaking. Finally, he kicked off his wet shoes, unlocked the door, and crept inside. When his eyes adjusted to the dim illumination from the streetlights outside, he draped his coat over the metal back of one of the bar stools so it would dry. The bottle of Pinot noir that he'd brought home for Linda two nights before stood empty on the counter. The bottle had still been almost full last night.

Linda never drank more than a glass of wine with dinner, maybe two if they attended a party. He frowned. Pulling out his phone, he activated the flashlight app and shone it across the counter, the dining table, the sofa. He found her phone next to the Blu-Ray remote and an empty wine glass on the coffee table. No calls made or received tonight. Searching her contacts, he came across a Seattle number labeled only "P." He checked the log and saw several calls from the day before, but they all registered as "missed." After copying the number into his own phone, he put hers back where he found it, stripped out of his wet clothes, wrapped himself in the quilt, and stretched out on the sofa.

Linda's head throbbed, her stomach churned, her throat hurt, her nose was still stuffed up, and she wished she hadn't woken up. Stumbling downstairs, she saw the empty quilt still spread across the sofa, but no other evidence Jason had come home to sleep. She found a cola in the fridge and swallowed two extra-strength acetaminophen. The label warned against taking more than six pills per day. She wondered what would happen if she consumed the entire bottle. Unfortunately, she'd probably just get sick. She needed to find something stronger.

After putting the wine glass in the dishwasher and tossing the bottle in the recycle bin, she checked her phone. No calls. She debated breakfast, but didn't think she would be able to keep anything down. For lack of something better to do, she went into the office to work.

Linda heard the front door open and looked at the clock. Except for bathroom breaks, she'd worked for nine hours straight. She debated whether she should emerge from the office until the smell of Chinese take away permeated the room and her stomach rumbled.

Stepping out of the office, she found Jason in the kitchen removing container after container from a large paper sack. He extracted two plates from the cabinet and put together mu shu chicken on each one, coating the pancake with sauce, filling it with the meat and vegetable mixture, tucking in the ends before rolling it up. Even when bringing home restaurant food, he chose something he would have to prepare for her. He arranged egg rolls, sweet and sour pork, shrimp with pea pods, orange chicken, and fried rice around the filled mu shu pancake. He handed her a plate and a set of paper-wrapped chopsticks, took the other for himself and sat down at the table.

Linda stood, the aroma of garlic, chilies, plum sauce, soy sauce, and fried breading steaming up from her plate, making her mouth water and her stomach grumble.

Jason broke his chopsticks apart and rubbed them together. "Sit. Eat. Knowing you, I'm guessing you haven't eaten all day, probably not since you made me breakfast yesterday."

Linda dropped into the chair across from him. She lifted an egg roll and dipped it into the hot mustard and sweet and sour sauce he'd mixed together in a bowl between them. The middle was still hot, but not enough to burn her tongue, and the spicy hot and tangy sweet of the combined sauces opened her sinuses. The first morsel woke her appetite and she shoveled food into her mouth as fast as she could pick it up with the chopsticks. Spices and flavors blended together, but gradually, the hollow feeling in her tummy subsided and she sat back satiated if not satisfied.

Jason still picked at the morsels on his plate, gripping them with the chopsticks and lifting them to his mouth individually rather than scooping them up together.

"Should I ask where you've been?"

He looked up, his eyes red rimmed, two days growth covering his face. "Should I ask what you've been doing?"

"Today? Working enough so I could take tomorrow off if I had a reason to."

"Why is sex maniac Phil coming to town?"

She closed her eyes and pressed her lips together.

"What reason are you looking for? I have classes to teach."

"Actually, you don't. It's Martin Luther King Day."

He cleared his throat until she looked up again and asked, "And last night? What were you doing while you drank almost an entire bottle of wine?"

"Mostly crying. Also, I knew it was the only way I'd get any sleep."

He pushed his plate away and folded his hands together, staring at them, avoiding her eyes. "But, you hurt me."

"Why do you think I've been sobbing my eyes out."

"Because you can't have your cake and eat it too?"

Linda shoved away from the table and tore up the stairs. The only thing worse than Jason's absence was his scorn. She threw herself across the un-made bed and sobbed into the comforter until she felt a weight on the mattress beside her and a hand on her back. Hoping, she lifted herself up on her elbows and rolled into his lap grabbing him around the waist, her cheek pressed against the rough denim of his jeans. For a moment, the muscles under her face tensed. Then they relaxed and she felt his hand on her head, his fingers running through her curls.

She inched closer so she could press her forehead against his stomach, pushing into the bit that pudged out. Taking a deep breath, she inhaled the scent of wet denim, the aroma of fried oil that clung to the fabric, but underneath it the smell of Irish Spring, garlic, and underwear that needed changing. Basking in his touch and his scent, she clung to him, hoping he wouldn't leave her and that he wouldn't make her choose.

He sighed. "I'm going to go back downstairs and put away the leftovers and take a shower. Since apparently neither of us has to get up early in the morning, maybe we should go see a movie or something?"

Anything to avoid talking. But she'd rather go see a movie with him than stay at home alone. "Sure."

They slipped back into their old routine. Linda was too terrified that Jason would leave her to force the conversation they needed to have. Her boss asked her to schedule a trip to Chicago, but understood when she claimed trauma made it impossible for her to travel. Sylvia only reminded her that the company had an EAP and a provider could be found in Port-land if she needed one.

Linda didn't know whether to be upset or relieved that she hadn't heard from Phil since the day after she returned to Oregon. Of course, she had ignored his calls that day and had made no effort to return them.

The monthly prescription arrived when the current bottle still contained four of the ten pills. It sat on the counter while they ate spaghetti carbonara and exchanged small talk about school, work, and their colleagues. The one name never mentioned loomed over every conversation.

Washing up, Jason pointed his chin at the white envelope. "Been two weeks. Think you're up to using one of those?"

Linda's throat closed and all she could squeak out was "Please."

Jason started the dishwasher and extracted the old bottle from the drawer where they kept all their pills. After he swallowed one, he pulled her into his arms, so her head rested against his shoulder, lifted her chin with two fingers and pressed his lips to hers. At first, he just kissed her, even though she opened her mouth to him. But soon his touch grew hungry and he hugged her tighter, his tongue exploring her mouth, his lips sucking gently on hers.

She lifted one leg over his, so she could grind herself on his thigh. He reached around and squeezed her rear, sending a charge of need through her that could only be satisfied with full body, skin-to-skin contact. She ripped his shirt open, not caring that one of the buttons tore free and skittered across the wooden floor.

He grabbed her hands. "I thought..." He pressed his lips together and planted them at the curve of her neck. Then he released her, took her hand, and led her up the stairs.

Nibbling on her ear, licking the length of her neck, he unfastened her blouse slowly, pushing one button through fabric at a time. He ran his hand over her exposed chest, dragging a finger between her breasts, while he reached behind her and unhooked her bra. Once he had her naked from the waist up, he drew her to him, holding her tight with an arm behind her back, fondling her breast with the other.

Linda sighed, her nipple hardening in his palm, her juices flowing, her pussy twitching in need.

Jason unbuttoned her jeans, reached behind her and swept away the blankets, then laid her gently back onto the sheets. As she crab-walked backwards on the bed, he pulled underwear, socks, and slippers off with her pants.

She reached up her arms and he stripped out of his own clothing, tossing it aside and falling on top of her. Wrapping her arms and legs around him, pulling him close, she kissed him, thrusting her tongue between his lips, pressing her breasts against his chest, reveling in his weight on top of her.

He pulled away from her lips, kissed his way down her neck, and licked each breast in turn, suckling softly on the nipple before moving on. When he'd lavished attention on both breasts, he ran his lips down her belly, pausing to tickle her navel with his tongue. Linda's chest heaved as her breathing came in gasps. Sliding off the bed to his knees on the carpet, he slowly dragged his tongue through her bush, and parted her lips with his fingers. He inhaled, then probed her labia with his tongue. With her heels on the edge of the bed, Linda pushed her hips toward him.

Jason chuckled and pulled away. She groaned in frustration. When she lowered her ass to the sheets again, he leaned in and licked the length of her inner lips, sending a quiver through her, making her clit ache for contact.

"Mmmmm." He pushed his tongue into her, tormenting her by staying away from where she needed him most.

"Please."

He chuckled and teased her, licking her everywhere but where she wanted him to. Lifting his head up, he licked her juices off his lips. She groaned, but he eased into her and rubbed his pelvic bone against her clit as he slid in and out. The tension built, and she reached around, grabbing his rear, pulling him harder and tighter against her. Finally, she came, shuddering against him, her clit quivering, longing for more. But as soon as she moaned with her climax, Jason released his hold over his own orgasm and cried out.

He stayed, resting his weight on forearms that were still wrapped around her back until he slipped out. Then he helped her reposition in the bed and lay down beside her with one arm across her chest under her breasts, and one leg between hers. Within minutes his breathing leveled out to the regular, heavy in and out of sleep. A tear crept from Linda's eye down her temple into her ear. She missed Phil so.

CHAPTER SIXTEEN

Linda took a day off to celebrate her birthday. Not that she had much to celebrate. She hadn't even spoken to Phil for three weeks, Jason still squelched any attempt to steer the conversation into treacherous waters, and she was horny as hell. Jason promised to take her to lunch, but she decided to accept Melinda and Joanne's offer of coffee and croissant while he taught his morning class.

She hadn't heard from him by the time her friends headed for the Max green line, so she returned to the condo. When she entered, the door slammed behind her, a big hand covered her mouth, and an arm gripped her waist in a vise-like grip. She panicked. *How did Phil get in? How will Jason react?*

But two other hands unfastened her blouse and she opened her eyes wide watching Jason pull buttons through fabric, a look of concentration on his face. She struggled, pushing first at the arm attached to the hand the kept her from crying out, then at the one pulling her tight against Phil's chest. Of course, she couldn't break free from his grip. And if Jason didn't object she didn't want to. Still, the struggle turned her on almost as much as Jason's hands against her skin. Pulling down her bra, he squeezed her breasts, pinching the nipple of one between his thumb and forefinger and biting the other.

With Phil still holding her in his iron grip, Jason released her breasts and unbuttoned her slacks, pulling them down over her hips, stripping off her panties, trouser socks, and pumps. Phil threw her over the sofa arm, unzipped, and jammed himself into her, using her hair to hold her in place.

Jason knelt on the sofa, his own pants and boxers missing, and forced her mouth open with his fingers pressing at the back of her jaw. With one hand he placed his limp member across her tongue. "If you bite me, bitch, I'll cut your face." His other hand reached forward and squeezed her breast again, pinching the nipple.

Linda sucked, running her tongue up and down the back of his penis. Phil slammed into her over and over again, jiggling her free breast and her belly, sending thrills to her G-spot that reverberated through her entire body. If Jason had been longer, she would have swallowed his glans when she came the first time, her entire body shaking.

Phil grasped her hips, keeping her still so he could plow into her. Holding on with one hand, he reached around with the other and diddled her clit, sending her into another paroxysm of pleasure. She closed her eyes and allowed all the physical sensations to run rampant, thrilled to have one of her favorite fantasies come to life. Her pussy ached, her clit throbbed, and soreness overwhelmed her nipple until Jason switched his torment to the other breast. One orgasm rolled into the next one and she couldn't distinguish them from each other. Jason finally got hard and almost immediately dribbled his salty semen into her mouth. After pounding into her for what must have been half an hour, Phil groaned and filled her pussy, holding her hips while he emptied himself into her, staying there until he softened.

When he released her, Linda fell to one side and would have landed on the floor if Phil hadn't grabbed her and eased her onto the sofa so she lay on her side, her head cradled in Jason's lap. Phil slid under her legs so she was stretched across the two of them, her pussy spasming, her tortured nipples throbbing, her clit quivering, her eyes rolled back in her head, her lips parted, still gasping for breath.

The hands of the two men she loved caressed her hips and toyed with her hair. Bliss.

When her breathing finally subsided to something closer to normal, Jason leaned over and whispered in her ear. "Happy birthday, my love."

She blinked her eyes open and slowly brought his chubby face into focus. "This must have been hard on you."

He pressed his lips together.

"Thank you my darling, you can't even imagine how much I enjoyed having both of you, how happy you've made me." She smiled and after a moment the corners of his mouth turned up slowly.

Phil stroked her calf. "Weren't we supposed to take this lovely lady out for a birthday lunch?"

"Only if you promise to do this to me again when we get back."

Jason frowned. "Twice, in one day, I'm not sure..."

Phil punched his shoulder. "Don't worry, Dude. I've got an idea."

Jason tilted his head and looked at the other man with a quizzical look.

Phil laughed. "Well, I can't exactly explain it in front of her, now can I?" He set Linda's feet on the floor. "Why don't you go upstairs, wash up, and dress up for a special treat?"

Jason helped Linda sit up on the sofa and Phil leaned over and whispered. "Dress sexy for us, from your skin outward."

The two men pulled Linda to her feet and she wobbled over toward the stairs. They laughed together.

"Are you sure you want more of this? You can barely walk now."

Linda couldn't even tell who spoke, but she nodded as she used the railing to pull herself up the stairs. In the bathroom, she splashed cold water on her face and used a washrag to clean the stickiness off her inner thighs and labia. She dug in her underwear drawer until she found a lacy black push up bra and matching thong. While searching, she caught her fingers on a black garter belt and she untangled it from her everyday cotton panties. She retrieved an unopened package of black silk stockings from the bottom of the drawer, and pulled them on over her legs. The fabric gliding across her skin made her feel sexy and the crotch of her thong got moist.

After slipping into a pair of three-inch, spiked heels — as high as she could manage to walk in for more than a few steps — she pushed aside garment after garment in her closet, looking for something worthy of her underwear. Back against the far side, she found a low-cut, snug, black spandex dress with a skirt that barely covered the tops of her stockings. Pulling it out, she remembered buying it back when she still thought she could revive Jason's interest in sex if she made herself more alluring. She sighed, but pulled the dress over her head. It hugged her curves and showed off the cleavage pushed up by the bra. Maybe now he could appreciate it instead of seeing it as a condemnation of his impotence.

When she sashayed down the stairs, Phil leaned against the end of the kitchen counter and Jason sat in one of the stools. They both whistled, although Jason's broke in the middle. "Wow. You're beautiful."

Phil punched Jason's shoulder. "Don't act so surprised, Dude. You live with this lovely lady, surely you appreciate how lucky you are to share your life with someone so gorgeous."

Linda looked at both of them fondly. She was the lucky one. If Jason had finally overcome his reluctance to share her with Phil, she would be the happiest woman in the world.

Jason helped her on with her leather coat and Phil opened the door for her. They walked down to the car. Linda had thought they were just going to Jake's Crawfish, but perhaps the two of them had decided to take her someplace else. Phil handed her into the front seat of the Subaru, then climbed into the back. Jason drove them a few blocks to the Smart Park.

Linda thought that silly, but then realized that walking that far in the shoes she wore would be painful at best. Jason wound his way up to the very top of the garage. Did he not want to be seen with the two of them? They could tell anyone they ran into that Phil was a friend from Seattle. When Phil handed our out of the car, she shrugged. They'd already made this the most memorable, thrilling birthday she had ever experienced. She wouldn't allow any quirks or confusion trouble her.

Once seated in a high-backed, wooden booth at Jake's, Linda understood some of Jason's concern. After she slid in, the waiter removed the place setting next to hers, leaving two opposite. Jason plopped down beside her, and put a hand on her thigh, as if claiming her. Phil bowed and took the seat opposite, moving one of the place settings back in front of Jason.

Although he rested his hand possessively on her leg, Jason didn't stroke her thigh or move high enough to determine that she wore stockings rather than panty hose. Phil's fingers would have discovered that she wore only a thong under her skirt before the waiter took their order.

"I think we need some oysters, don't you Dude?" Phil winked across the table.

Jason managed half a smile. "Which kind?"

Phil chuckled. "Maybe we should try the combination."

Jason added orders of salmon cakes, steamed Manila clams, and fried calamari to the two Oyster Combination plates Phil told the waiter to bring.

The raw oysters arrived quickly and Jason added just a hint of horse-radish before holding one up to her lips. She tilted her head back and he poured the delicious slipperiness into her mouth, then indulged in one himself. Phil covered his in Tabasco sauce before swallowing it and she forced herself not to grimace.

They had emptied the plate by the time the hot appetizers appeared. Jason fed her bits of salmon and clams and squid, the latter delicately fried in a panko crust that melted on her tongue, while Phil ran his feet up the inside of her leg and pressed his toes against the thin fabric of her thong. She wondered if she would be leaving the restaurant with a damp spot on the back of her skirt. The flavors blended together in a delicious combi-nation, almost as appealing as the male fusion presented by the two men sharing food with her.

Jason, reliable and prosaic as Phil was sexy and dangerous made a perfect combination for someone who wanted the best of both worlds. She slid one shoe off and moved her toes up Phil's calf while massaging the inside of Jason's thigh with her hand.

When the waiter cleared the plates, they decided to forgo entrees and go straight to dessert. Linda ordered the chocolate cups filled with mousse. Jason shared his bread pudding with her and Phil leaned over to feed her tastes of his cheesecake. Then they insisted she eat all the dark chocolate, although they did help themselves to her mousse filling.

Phil leaned forward and whispered across the table. "Not that you need it, but I know for a fact that chocolate is an aphrodisiac for women."

Jason chuckled and Phil winked. When the check came, Linda excused herself and went to the restroom, unwilling to watch them tussle over the bill. By the time she returned, the leather folder had disappeared and she didn't ask how they'd resolved the issue.

Dinner guests filled the tables by the time they left the restaurant, and darkness had descended on the city. The men walked on either side of her, and Linda put her arms through theirs. They were two blocks from the parking garage when Phil said, "I have to run a quick errand. I'll meet you two back at the condo if that's okay?"

"Sure," Linda said without pausing. She needed to get off the heels and was grateful Jason had decided to drive, cutting the distance she had to walk back to the condo in half. By the time they reached the top level, no cars were visible.

They exited the elevator and made their way toward the massive pillar supporting the roof that Jason had parked behind. As she tottered out of the well-lit area surrounding the elevator, dark cloth smashed against her face and was pulled over her head. An arm grabbed her around her waist jerking her back up against a rock hard chest. A hand held the hood taut over her mouth, forcing an attached gag between her lips.

CHAPTER SEVENTEEN

Linda struggled, her chest tightening, her pulse racing. Someone was carjacking, robbing, kidnapping them. *But, why? Where's Jason?* She grabbed at the steel band gripping her waist with both hands, but couldn't budge it. She kicked backward, aiming the stiletto where she thought a shin should be. The arm lifted her off the ground and her feet only encountered air.

Gradually a familiar scent penetrated the hood. *Phil.* Linda took a deep breath. She continued to struggle, but panic no longer made her heart thump in her ears. She heard the beep of the door alarm and the hatch raise on the back of the Subaru. Phil, *it has to be Phil*, forced her face down onto the rubber mat covering the back, tightened the hood so she couldn't dislodge the gag, and pulled her hands behind her back. Rope bound her wrists and ankles, she was shoved further in, and a blanket was tossed over her. She heard the window shade sound of the cargo cover pulling over her and the slam of the hatch back.

Only one car door opened and then slammed shut. What had happened to Jason? Had Phil stuffed her in the back of her own car or had a criminal beaten up Jason and kidnapped her? Bile rose in Linda's throat. She should have struggled harder. She twisted her wrists, but that just tightened the ropes and she had to stop before she cut off the circulation. The car jerked her from side to side as it was driven around and around down the exit ramp. She stopped breathing to listen when they paused to pay for the parking, but the driver didn't respond verbally to the clerk's greeting.

When the car pulled away, Linda gasped for breath. She should have screamed. But what if Phil was driving? If he was, where was Jason? She renewed her struggles and got tangled in the blanket.

The car drove much longer than it should have to take them back to the condo, even during rush hour traffic. It stopped and started, stopped and started, sometimes for a few seconds, sometimes for several long minutes. She needed to get free. If she brought her hands down so she could put her legs through them, then she could see how to remove the rope. Linda couldn't get them past her ass, her rear end too big and her wrists tied too tightly.

Finally the car stopped and the driver's side door opened. She heard scuffling and breathing, then it slammed shut and the hatch opened, letting in cold air.

A deep voice said "Well there. Thanks fer making my job easy and wrapping yooself up in the blanket." He pulled her from the station wagon, tossed her over his shoulder, and slammed the hatch closed. Linda's head hung down his back and he held her knees against his chest. The car lock beeped twice. Why would a kidnapper lock the car? It had to be Phil. But where was Jason?

Linda struggled to get off the man's shoulder.

"Settle down ya stupid dame. Ya fall off my shoulder, ya gonna crack yer head open on the cement. Boss ain't lookin' for me to bring him a corpse, tonight."

Linda sobbed. The voice, the accent, couldn't be Phil. And what had this monster done to Jason? And who was the Boss and what did he want with her?

The man walked up a series of steps, cement by the sound. Her weight didn't seem to slow him down. She heard a door open and slam shut, more stairs, and another door. The man shifted her weight and she rolled over and over as he poured her out of the blanket onto the floor. "I brotcha a present, Boss,"

Two hands under her armpits lifted her and positioned her on her knees. The hood was pulled off and Linda blinked in the bright light. Jason sat in the recliner wearing the silk robe she had bought him to use when he traveled. It was open to show he wore nothing underneath it. He had a small leather whip with a dozen falls in one hand and a high ball glass filled with what looked like whiskey in his other. He gripped an unlit stogie between his teeth. The curtains, open when they left, had all been drawn.

"Youse knows I don't like no gift wrapping."

Hands under her armpits lifted her to her feet and she saw a hunting knife out of the corner of her right eye.

"Please, don't hurt me." The words barely made it through parched lips and her voice cracked. One hand pulled the neckline of her dress away from her chest and the other brought the knife down to slice through the fabric exposing her lingerie.

Jason moved the stogie from one side of his mouth to the other without using his hands. "Nice. Bring it here."

The hands pushed Linda, forcing her to jump forward. Jason set the glass on the table next to his chair, reached up, and forced one finger under her thong. "What a slut." He patted his leg and Linda was pushed over his lap. With three more slices, her dress was ripped from her body and she lay across Jason's legs with her naked ass, framed by black garters, in the air.

The whip stung as the thongs struck her flesh and her pussy gushed. Someone jammed a plastic cock into her and Jason threw the whip again and again until she shrieked, coming so hard she almost rolled off Jason's lap. He lay the whip down across her naked back and caressed her ass.

"I likes this one. You can have a piece of it if you want, as a reward for your soivice."

"Thanks, Boss," the deep gruff voice said.

Linda felt the knife against her ankles then the ropes fell off. A hand on either side of her waist plucked her off Jason's lap and positioned her on her hands and knees in front of him. A chest was plastered against her back and a hard cock pushed at her behind. Two hands grabbed her breasts, twisting the nipples in opposite directions. The chest leaned forward, pressing her face into Jason's lap. She licked at his limp cock and he grabbed her hair holding her face to his crotch.

Slick fingers lubed her asshole and the huge hard cock slid inside, pressing against the plastic one still in her pussy. Linda came again, shuddering against the chest still pressed to her back.

Linda tried to remember Jason's cock, stabbing at it with her tongue, sucking the glans into her mouth when she had enough breath to do so. But the cock slamming in and out of her ass, the dildo up her pussy, the hands massaging her breasts, the finger tweaking her clit overwhelmed her with sensation, making it hard for her to concentrate enough give Jason more than perfunctory attention.

She groaned and came again, harder. Soon they had her in the same euphoric, non-stop orgasmic state they had driven her to earlier. Linda gave up and let them take over. Phil had to pull her hips back on his cock and Jason rubbed his against her lips. When Phil finally shot his load into her ass, Linda couldn't move. The moment he pulled out and released her, she fell over on her side.

"I think we may have finally found her satiation point," Phil said in his normal voice.

"You mostly." Jason sounded peeved.

Linda couldn't voice an opinion. Every part of her body reverberated in post-orgasmic bliss.

"*We* should put her to bed." Phil pulled Linda off the floor and lifted her in his arms.

Jason led the way to their bedroom and pulled back the covers. "You can sleep on the sofa if you want."

"Thanks." Linda heard Phil on the stairs and then water running in the bathroom. She fell asleep before Jason returned to their bed.

CHAPTER EIGHTEEN

Linda woke to find Jason standing over her dressed in his professor's uniform of blue Dockers, navy sweater, and light blue shirt. Daylight peeped between the curtain halves. "I have to go to school. I'll be back around four. If you fuck Phil while I'm gone, I don't want to know anything about it. And please, not in our bed." He leaned over and kissed her forehead, turned, and disappeared down the stairs.

Although his words seemed somewhat out of character, she found his easy return to routine reassuring. She stretched and debated going back to sleep or venturing downstairs to find Phil. Her pussy was still sore from the hammering she'd received the night before. But, she threw off the covers, stuck her feet into her slippers, and headed for the bathroom. Sore or not, she could never be sure when she would see Phil again. And, not having to sneak around behind Jason's back made sex with Phil even more delicious.

When she padded downstairs, wearing only a silky black slip and her pink terry cloth slippers, the sofa was empty, the bathroom door open. She saw no sign of Phil. She sighed and stood on the bottom step, trying to decide if she should make breakfast or get dressed first. A box from Nuvrei Pastries stood in front of the coffee pot which exuded the aroma of fresh brew. Jason must have made coffee and run over to the bakery before he left for school, asserting his role as the one who nurtured her. She'd slept so soundly, she hadn't even realized he had gotten out of bed.

Smiling at the memory of the delights her body had experienced the day before, she stepped down and approached the kitchen, wondering what Jason bought to tempt her. She flipped open the box, delighted to see a half dozen almond croissants, and opened the cabinet to retrieve a mug for coffee. Two hands grabbed her breasts and hot lips nibbled at her neck.

"You taste good enough for me. Who needs breakfast?"

Linda leaned back against his naked chest. She didn't have the energy to struggle. Phil turned her around, pulled her close to him with one arm around her waist and grabbed a fistful of hair with the other hand. He pulled her head back and took possession of her mouth. His tongue thrust between her parted lips and she sucked on it hungrily.

The hand at her waist slid down to her ass, squeezing her globes, pulling her hips against his already sheathed erection. Linda panted and she could feel her insides melting. Phil released her hair, but not her lips, scooped her up into his arms, and brought her to the sofa. He laid her down, spread her legs with his knee, and plunged inside her. She moaned. Soreness quickly gave way to the tightness that made her breath come in quick gasps. He leaned forward, pulled her slip down, and sucked gently on her tender nipples, alternating between them, teasing them with his tongue until she came.

Although he ground his pelvis into her clit with each thrust, Phil seemed to understand that she needed a break after the intensity of the day before. He was uncharacteristically almost gentle, even a bit tender, although she wouldn't go so far as to describe the sex as lovemaking.

When he filled the condom, he removed it and dropped it in a small paper bag. He grinned. "I'm guessing Jason would prefer not to see evidence."

Phil left Linda floating in post-orgasmic euphoria and returned with a cup of coffee and two of the croissants on a plate. He helped her sit up and fed her bits of one pastry while eating the other. When the plate was empty, he carefully licked the crumbs from her chest, breasts, and belly. By then he knelt on the floor in front of her, her legs spread, the back of her knees resting on his shoulders.

"And, for dessert..." He dove in, licking the insides of her outer lips then pressing his tongue into her folds, exploring, teasing, tantalizing.

After she came and came and came, Phil rested his cheek on her belly. "I do love you, Linda. I hope you know that."

Her breath caught in her throat. Her brain screamed that she shouldn't listen to love declarations from a naked man on his knees in the living room she shared with her husband while he met with students and taught class. But, her heart responded. "I love you too. Not the same way I love Jason..."

"Of course not. I wouldn't want you to love me the way you love him." He lifted her head and grinned at her. "I'd get bored quickly in that kind of relationship." He kissed her belly. "I need a shower. Care to join me?"

Linda nodded and he lifted her to her feet. She followed him into the bathroom and waited while he turned on and adjusted the water. With one hand he pulled back the shower curtain and put the other across his waist and bowed. "After you my dear."

Dropping her slip on the floor, Linda stepped over the side of the tub, moved toward the hot water, and turned her face up to let it stream over her. Phil wrapped his arms around her, one hand rubbing the bar of lavender-scented soap against her heated skin. Her breasts had never been cleaner. When he'd soaped her from neck to crotch, he turned her around, bent his knees, and rubbed his chest against hers. "Who needs a washcloth?" He grinned and kissed her, the water streaming through their hair. Slowly, he caressed her back and ass with the soap, then brought it around and lathered her bush. If he didn't have one arm around her back, she would have fallen against the taps. Her knees trembled and she felt unsteady on her feet.

Phil pulled the shower head from its bracket and rinsed Linda's skin. He paused before spraying between her legs, switching it to the massage setting. Holding her lips open with two fingers, he aimed the pulsating bursts of water at her clit. Linda clung to his shoulders as her body trembled and her knees refused to support her.

After he returned the shower head to its bracket, Phil helped her down to her knees and handed her the soap. She smiled and applied it to his skin, starting at his waist. After rubbing the ripped muscles of his abdomen, she guided the soap down his powerful thighs, ignoring the erection poking at her. Only after she had soaped his legs, ass and the tops of his feet, did she turn her attention to the heavy sacs. Gently, she teased them with the soap, holding each in one hand while she ran the edge of the bar across the skin. Finally, she moved to the massive penis that jutted out toward her mouth.

She rubbed the bar in both hands until she got bubbles and handed it to Phil. With one hand on either side, her fingers laced together on top her palms on the bottom, she slowly moved up and down the silky skin, slicking it in soap bubbles. Phil gasped, but kept still, the hot water pouring down his chest to splash onto her hands. When all the soap washed away, Linda took the glans into her mouth and ran her tongue around it, tasting the residual lavender of the soap over his musk. Keeping her lips tight against his shaft, she slid them down toward the dark, curly, soap-scented triangle of hair and back.

The smell of vanilla competed with the lavender as Phil massaged shampoo into her hair. Linda would have laughed if her mouth wasn't full. While he washed and rinsed her hair, she weighed his balls in one hand and gripped his ass cheek with the other, pulling him in and out of her mouth, keeping her tongue tight against his pole until her jaw ached and he finally emptied himself into her throat.

Phil leaned down and brought her back up to her feet, holding her tight, her face resting against his chest, the water cascading over her head. When the water started to cool, Phil turned it off, and reached for one of the towels hanging from the wall rack. He vigorously rubbed her hair dry, then gently patted every inch of her skin, before wrapping the towel around her and reaching for a second.

When they emerged from the bathroom, clouds of steam billowing out with them, Linda saw the clock over the fireplace. "It's three thirty. We'd better get dressed."

"Go on up." Phil swatted her ass. "I'll clean up down here."

When Linda came back down the stairs, wearing jeans and a sweater, only the lingering scent of lavender and vanilla gave evidence of how they had spent the day. Phil poured them both another cup of coffee and they were sitting at the counter when Jason fumbled through the door with his satchel and two bags of groceries. Phil jumped up to help him and then started unpacking the cloth bags.

Jason hung his coat in the closet. "The market had fresh scallops. Thought I'd make them for dinner."

Phil stared at the array of ingredients on the counter — two onions, a flower of garlic, fresh fettuccine, tomatoes, onions, two bottles of Pinot gris, a baguette, packages of basil, thyme, and grated Parmesan, and two tubs of scallops — and then at Jason. "I'm impressed, Dude. I wouldn't have any idea how to make a meal out of all this. But, I'm happy to help if you'll tell me what to do."

Jason pulled butter and olive oil from the fridge. "Thanks, but in the kitchen I prefer to work alone."

Linda tried to judge how he was managing emotionally, but his voice was neutral.

Phil joined Linda at the counter and tried to make small talk. At first only Linda responded, until he asked Jason what he thought of Dirty Martini. An hour and a half later, the pasta bubbled in a pot of water and sinfully rich aromas emerged from the largest skillet they owned. Jason had rolled up his sleeves and shed his sweater. He only used a third of the Pinot to cook with and split the rest of the bottle between them.

Linda sipped at the fruity wine and resisted pinching herself to see if she was dreaming. If she was asleep, she didn't want to wake up. The two men she adored were comparing the indie music scene in Portland and Seattle while Jason set the table and Phil opened the second bottle of Pinot.

She moved to the table when Jason held out a chair for her and let him refill her wine glass. After dinner, they retired to the living room and nibbled on the truffles he had bought a few days before while sipping glasses of tawny port. Jason had her feet in his lap, massaging first one and then the other. Phil stood behind her, rubbing her shoulders.

"You two are spoiling me. I could get very used to this."

"Unfortunately, we'd better call it a night." Jason put her slippers back on. "Tomorrow's my morning class."

She kissed Phil good night, staggered toward the stairs, and realized that she'd managed to get tipsy. Jason had to help her up to the bedroom. When she crawled into bed, he pulled her into his arms and kissed her, his mouth closed. But his lips wandered down her chin and along her neck, to her breasts. She sighed contentedly when he found her nipple and sucked on it. She hadn't seen him take a pill and knew he probably couldn't handle it two days in a row anyway, but she couldn't stop her body from responding to his caresses.

Lifting her hips slightly from the bed, she moaned. Jason obliged, dragging his lips across her belly to her bush. Although he couldn't match Phil for technique or stamina, Jason persisted, licking her nub and sucking on it until the tension finally built and she screamed, the orgasm shuddering through her. Jason crawled up and rested his head next to hers on the pillow. She fell asleep with his arm across her waist.

Jason had left when Linda dragged herself out of bed the next morning and went in search of aspirin. She came downstairs to find a note from Phil on the counter.

"Now I know why Jason said he didn't want to know what you and I were doing. I've taken a room across the river at the Crowne Plaza. Always thought I wasn't the jealous type, but I can't bear listening to you make love to him. Don't know when he gets home today, but if you've time before he does, let me know."

Linda crumbled the note and poured herself a cup of coffee. After taking two days off she should get some work done, but Phil's invitation made her clit throb with need. She sent him a text, threw on some clothes, and scurried down to the car. When she pulled into the hotel parking lot, she had received a response from Phil containing only a number.

She took the elevator to the seventh floor and knocked on room 725.

The force of her taps pushed the door ajar. "Phil?" With one finger, she nudged the door until it was fully open. All she could see was the vanity sink outside the bathroom door on her right and the end of a king bed beyond that. The desk in the corner had nothing on it except the usual hotel paraphernalia. Maybe she had the wrong room. Linda turned back toward the empty corridor and a hand clamped over her mouth and a muscular arm encircled her waist, pulling her backwards into the room. The door was kicked closed and Linda was tossed face down on the bed.

She tried to push herself up with her arms, but a crushing weight fell on her, forcing her to exhale. Hands slid under her body and clenched her breasts. Hot breath on her neck sent a chill down her spine. A finger forced its way between her legs, pushed aside the crotch of her panties, and was put in front of her nose, covered in her own juices. "You're such a slut, gods how I love your insatiable appetite."

Phil eased onto his side, pushed her skirt up and pulled her panties down. He spanked her until her ass was warm and she wriggled with need. Grabbing the pillows, he shoved them under her pelvis, forcing her ass up in the air. He slammed into her so hard the bed shook and the headboard creaked. His fingers digging into her hips, his balls slapping her thighs, he fucked her hard and long.

Except for the two times the three of them were together, Jason always made love to her. And except for yesterday and once when he visited the apartment for the first time, Phil always fucked her. She needed both.

Since Phil hadn't used a condom, Linda showered before she got dressed to return home. She locked the bathroom door. Although she would have loved to have Phil join her, she needed to get back before Jason did.

Phil kissed her goodbye, pressing her body against the wall with his. "I've gotten rather behind at work. I'm going to stay in and try to catch up tonight. Let's all get together tomorrow?"

She kissed his chin. "Why don't you come over for brunch. I'll text you what time after I talk to Jason."

CHAPTER NINETEEN

In the morning, Jason didn't feel like cooking, so he dashed out for bagels, smoked salmon, cream cheese, tomatoes, and onions. He had just finished slicing and arranging it all on a tray when Phil knocked. He kissed her chastely on the lips — mouth closed — and set a plastic container of grapes and cut up melon and pineapple in the center of the table before hanging his leather jacket in the closet. "Brought some fruit."

Jason pushed Phil's fruit to one side and set his platter in its place. After adding the coffee carafe, plates, mugs, napkins, and flatware, he held out Linda's chair and sat next to her.

No one spoke until they had filled their plates. Jason nudged a piece of salmon around his plate with his fork. "I can't do this."

Tears sprung to Linda's eyes and she set the bagel smeared with cream cheese back on her plate.

Jason took a sip of his coffee. "I've tried to understand. I recognize I can't meet your sexual needs." He turned to Linda. "But, I'm your husband, damn it. If that's not important to you anymore, perhaps we should just go our separate ways."

Linda closed her eyes, unable to stand the accusation in Jason's eyes. "I don't want to leave you. I love you." She wiped away a tear.

"Then be my wife, not his floozy." Jason tipped his cup in Phil's direction.

"Please, I'm begging you, don't make me choose between you. I love you both."

Phil set his fork down and swallowed whatever he had put in his mouth. "Marriage doesn't have to mean monogamy. I've always been poly, even when I was married."

Jason set his cup down so hard, coffee sploshed onto his placemat. "You have a lot of nerve comparing your marriage with mine. Your wife's lover was another woman and I doubt if they made you feel sexually inadequate."

Phil set his hands flat on the table. "This isn't just about sex. If it was, we wouldn't need to have this conversation. Some people were meant to mate with only one person at a time, but that's not as common as the religious zealots would have you believe. More marriages probably would survive longer if there was less stigma against polyamory."

"That word's a problem in and of itself. You're combining Latin and Greek." Jason used his napkin to wipe up the spilled coffee. "It doesn't work and neither do poly relationships, for the most part."

Phil chuckled. "And, you know this how? Most poly people aren't able to be open about it. But which would you prefer," he leaned forward slightly, "that Linda have a long-term relationship with someone who loves her, cares about her, and respects your marriage or that she cheats behind your back with whoever happens to be available at the time?"

"I'm not a..." Linda broke off realizing she was a cheater. She hadn't told Jason about her relationship with Phil until they'd been involved for months.

Jason spread cream cheese on a bagel half, ignoring the one missing a single bite on his plate. "If you're willing to blow nineteen and a half years of marriage for hot sex, you have every right to do so." He jammed the knife back into the cream cheese. "But, you don't have the right to expect me to wait at home twiddling my thumbs while this guy fucks your brains out."

Phil sighed. "You're used to Linda being in Chicago at least one week a month. What did you do while she was gone before I came into the picture?"

Jason speared a piece of pineapple from the fruit tray, but then set it down on his plate. "What does that have to do with anything? She was working and I didn't have to wonder how many times you 'raped' her." He lifted his fingers and pulled air quotes.

"Please, stop." Tears streamed down Linda's face. "I can't, I can't..." She pushed herself away from the table and ran up the stairs, throwing herself into the armchair and pulling her knees against her breasts. She could hear the two men's voices, but not their words. Reaching to the ottoman, she grabbed the throw and pulled it up over herself to her chin. The tone of the voices became angrier and she covered her head, sobbing into her shirt sleeve. She wished the condo was up higher so she could just jump off the balcony and make the voices stop.

The front door slamming preceded the sound of footsteps trudging up the stairs. Linda pushed herself off the chair and threw herself into the bathroom, slamming the door and pressing the lock closed. She splashed cold water on her face but sobs continued to shake her upper body. Leaning against the door, she slid to the tile of the floor and sat there with her head in her hands until her tears dried up. Hiccoughs combined with snot made breathing difficult.

After blowing her nose until she could breathe through it, Linda washed her face which did nothing to alleviate her red eyes and the puffiness that surrounded them. She cracked the bathroom door and listened. The only sounds were from outside. Creeping into the bedroom, she saw no evidence Jason had taken anything. Downstairs, the food had been put away and the dishwasher was running. She stumbled into her office, booted up her computer, and tackled the hundreds of e-mails that had accumulated in the past three days.

Linda heard the front door open then slam closed and the bolt turn. In the middle of composing an e-mail to Sylvia, she didn't want to lose her train of thought. She was vaguely aware of the kitchen light turning on then off and footsteps on the stairs.

When she finally emerged from the office, the kitchen clock said eleven forty-five. She didn't believe it until she confirmed it on her cell. At least neither of them had to work in the morning. Linda's stomach grumbled and she realized she hadn't eaten anything since the mouthful she'd consumed before all hell broke out at the breakfast table. Rummaging in the fridge, she found the leftovers and made herself a sandwich. She ate it standing up over the sink like some stereotypical bachelor. *What you have to look forward to if Jason leaves you.* She washed it down with what was left of the Pinot gris, drinking straight from the bottle, and went upstairs. Jason slept on his side, his back to where she should be, as close to his edge of the bed as he could get without falling off.

Tears spilled from Linda's eyes. She couldn't blame the man after what she had done. But, he didn't understand her needs and couldn't fill them. Hiding in the bathroom again, Linda tried to brush her teeth. But the salmon threatened to come back up and she settled for rinsing with mouthwash. Flipping off the light, she grabbed the throw from the floor in front of the ottoman, and took it downstairs. Still fully dressed, she wrapped it around herself, pulled the quilt Phil had used over her head and fell onto the sofa. Wine combined with exhaustion put her to sleep before she soaked her sleeve with tears.

"You didn't have to sleep on the sofa."

Linda pushed off the comforter and tried to rub out the crick in her neck. She heard the clatter of dishes in the kitchen.

"I made a mushroom frittata if you want some."

The aroma of coffee laced with onions and mushrooms cooked in butter overwhelmed her and she had to dash to the bathroom. Only bile emerged, but her stomach continued to heave. When she finally stood up to splash water on her face, Jason stood in the doorway with a glass of cola.

"Here, this will settle your stomach. Then you can decide if you want anything to eat." His face was drawn and pale and dark shadows surrounded his eyes. "I can make you some dry toast or maybe some oatmeal. I'll put the frittata in the fridge and you can have it later."

He turned on his heel and left her standing at the sink, holding the glass. She sat on the toilet and sipped at the sickeningly sweet bubbles. Linda never drank soda except when she was sick. Jason said it was his mother's remedy and he'd taught her to use it for stomach ailments when they first started dating.

When she emerged from the bathroom, the kitchen was empty. A piece of toast sat on a plate on the counter. She caught movement out of the corner of her eye and saw Jason standing on the deck, watching the river. Pulling on her coat, she opened the sliding glass door just far enough to step outside and join him.

He leaned on the metal railing and peered through the trees at the *Spirit of Portland* motoring by. "I'm going to miss this view."

"There's no reason for you to leave." She longed to put her arms around him, but couldn't bear even the thought of him rejecting her.

He shrugged. "Even if you move up to Seattle to be closer to Phil, I don't think I could stay here. Too many memories."

"Please don't leave me." Linda sobbed.

Turning, he leaned his back against the railing. "*If* you were willing to give up Phil to stay with me, how could I ever trust you again?" He crossed his arms over his chest. "You've gotten a taste of what you consider great sex, something I can never give you again. I think you forgot what it was like, that's why you stayed monogamous with me before ... assuming Phil is your first affair. But now that you've remembered, now that..." He cleared his throat.

Linda sank into one of the cushioned metal chairs that faced the river, ignoring the cold damp seeping through her jeans. "It was never just about sex. And the sex is nothing like what you and I share. You and I make love. Phil and I have sex. I don't want to give up making love to you. That's what you don't seem to understand. More than anything else, I love you both in different ways. Just like making love to you is different than having sex with Phil. But, I can't choose between you. I don't want to..."

"You keep saying you can't choose. So, I'm making the choice for you. I'll move out as soon as I find a place to live."

Linda flung herself from the chair to where Jason stood, throwing her arms around his waist, clinging to him. "No. God, no. Please, don't leave me. I love you. I don't want... can't live with Phil. I want to stay with you."

He pushed at her shoulders, forcing her to release him. "Are you willing to stop seeing Phil? To be monogamous? I'm not saying that's even a solution, I still have to learn to trust you again. But, if he stays involved in your life in any way, I can't."

Linda sank to the plastic composite boards of the deck, and clutched Jason around the knees. Her tears wet his khaki pants.

He didn't push her away, but his hands stayed on the railing.

She sniveled. "You have to tell him."

"That's really not appropriate. You can send him an e-mail."

Her shoulders shook. He toyed with a strand of her hair. "I love you Linda, more than you can imagine. But, I can't, I'm sorry, I just can't share you."

She released him and pushed herself to her feet. "If you really loved me you wouldn't make me choose."

Inside, she shed her coat, dumped it on the sofa, and stumbled into the office. The screen was blurry when she booted her computer. Her message was simple.

Phil:
    Jason will leave me if I see you again.
    I'm sorry. I'll miss you.
Linda

After she hit the send button, sobs doubled her over. She pushed the keyboard to one side so it wouldn't get wet and rested her head on the cool laminate surface of her desk.

She didn't know how long Jason had been standing behind her, didn't realize he was there until he stroked her hair. "Thank you. I'll do my best to make sure you don't regret your decision."

But, Linda already did.

CHAPTER TWENTY

Monday morning Linda polished her resume and sent it off to the nine people who had approached her about working for them over the past three years. They all wrote back by the end of the day saying that they wished they could offer her a position, but their firms just weren't hiring and, given the economy, they couldn't anticipate any openings in the coming year.

A few days later, Jason brought home a package wrapped in shiny black paper with a silver bow and set it on Linda's desk. She unwrapped it to find the box contained an eight-inch long, three-inch thick, pink dildo.

"I know I'm not as well endowed as Phil. I'm hoping this will help. It has a vibrator function and the clerk said it's a very popular model, especially for women who like big dicks."

Sitting back in her chair, she just stared at it.

Jason cleared his throat. "You can use it whenever you like, don't have to worry if I've taken my pill, or wait for someone else to take care of your needs."

For all his claim of loving her, Jason didn't seem to understand anything about her desires as a woman, her fantasies, her appetites. She didn't want a dildo. She needed a man, one who could throw her down, rip off her clothes, spank her, and fuck her until she was too sore to walk.

When she took a break for lunch the next day, Linda decided to give the toy a fair shot. Jason was trying, even if his approach was all wrong. She drew the bedroom curtains and dumped her clothes in the chair. Stretching out on her side of the bed, she closed her eyes and imagined Phil's hand across her mouth, his teeth on her nipple, his tongue on her clit. She flipped the on button and rubbed the buzzing plastic across her breasts, down her belly, and into her bush. With two fingers, she held her lips open so she could press it against her clit. Her fingers touched dry flesh, eliminating any thought of trying to insert it.

Licking her lips, she tried to remember how it felt when Phil turned her over his knee and spanked her butt until she could feel the redness. She pressed her lips together imagining his wonderfully thick cock pushing against her cheeks, probing her pussy, and ramming her ass. Pushing the buzzing glans of the fake dick against her clit as hard as she could with one hand, she squeezed her tit with the other. She couldn't pinch her nipple as hard as Phil did, but at least the sensation triggered some moisture.

Sliding the dildo back and forth on her clit seemed to work better than just holding it tightly. She tried to ease it into her pussy, but the silicone felt nothing like flesh. It was too big and she was too dry for it to prompt any pleasurable sensations. After about half an hour, she managed to make herself come, once. And the orgasm felt more like the tension just stopped than the explosions Phil precipitated or even the shuddering release when Jason made love to her.

With nothing to recover from, Linda pushed herself off the bed and pulled her clothing back on. She washed off the toy, not that there was much on it, and stashed it in the drawer of her nightstand. She went downstairs even more horny than when she had climbed up them. Eventually, she hoped, Jason would want to do more than sleep in their bed. For years that had been enough.

She sat down at her desk and sobbed. *No, it never was.* Even before she met Phil, she was always hot and bothered, feeling guilty for wanting so much more than her husband could ever give her. From the beginning, Phil had sensed her need and worked hard to fill it — and her. It took her an entire box of tissues to get through the rest of the afternoon, reading every e-mail, every memo at least twice because she had difficulty seeing through the blur of her tears.

Working fifty or sixty hours a week, Linda communicated as much as she could via phone and used video teleconferencing whenever possible. But, after two months the messages from Sylvia asking when she would make her next trip to Chicago became more and more insistent. Finally, she broached the possibility of a business trip with Jason.

"Sylvia needs me to come in to the office for a few days." Linda sat at the counter, trying to sound casual, but out of Jason's sight, she twisted the corner of her sweater into a wrinkled knot.

Jason slammed his knife flat onto the plastic cutting board and turned around to the stove. After flipping off the burners, he stomped out of the condo, slamming the door behind him. Linda wept. It seemed that's what she did most these days: cry, sob, bawl, whimper, and wail. She slid off the stool and ventured around the counter into the kitchen. The frying pan was full of half cooked bits of onion and, from the aroma garlic, frying in olive oil. She stirred the large sauce pot on the back burner and took a whiff. Chicken stock. The spoon didn't turn up anything solid. On the counter a half cut up bell pepper sat next to two tomatoes and a carton of crimini mushrooms. Jason also had taken a bag of flour from the pantry and it stood next to an empty bowl. She had no idea what he planned to make. Linda returned to her desk and spent the next three hours pursuing job listings on LinkedIn and craigslist.

Jason still hadn't come back home when she gave up and returned to the kitchen. The sauce pot was now full of cold jelly, the vegetables on the counter looked dried up, and the mess in the frying pan smelled putrid rather than enticing. Linda put the flour and mushrooms away and poured the congealed stock into the garbage disposal. While it was running, she filled the compost bin with everything else and put the pots in the dishwasher.

She paced back and forth between the living room and her office. She checked her cell every five minutes to make sure she hadn't missed a phone call or text. When she tried to sit down and read e-mail or even the news sites, her attention wandered. What would Phil do if she begged him to take her in? Would Carol even accept her living in the same city? How would Jason react if she left? Maybe she should move back to Ohio and see if her parents had mellowed any in their old age. Assuming they were still alive. If Jason divorced her, they could scold her and say they told her so. She wondered if her sister's order would take someone her age. If she was going to be celibate anyway, why not become a nun?

Finally just before midnight, Linda crawled into bed and cried herself to sleep. At least she didn't have to restrain herself to prevent Jason from hearing her weep. She howled into the pillow until her throat was sore and her eyes puffy.

She woke an hour before the alarm was set to go off. Jason clung to his side of the bed, his back to her, his head under the pillow.

Linda hadn't left the condo in two months. She didn't even go out onto the deck, unwilling to acknowledge Spring and all its beauty. The black and white decor of the condo suited her mood better than the riot of blooming color she would find if she ventured outside. She missed Phil. She longed to have sex. Jason had one half empty and two unopened bottles in the kitchen drawer. He hadn't made love to her since she saw Phil for the last time. He rarely even kissed her, never reached for her hand at night. He slept on the far side of the bed, clinging to the edge as if letting go would drag him back into her arms. He locked the door whenever he used the bathroom.

Once or twice, Linda had reached across the table or tried to put her arms around him when he was cooking dinner. He pulled away or dodged her touch. She no longer tried to hide her puffy eyes and swollen nose from him. Her tears were as much a result of her mourning what she had lost with Jason as for the aching hole Phil's absence left in her heart. Jason had asked her to choose, but he hadn't warned her that choosing him meant having neither.

Phil had never responded to her e-mail, although she occasionally saw his work address copied on company correspondence. The first time she had been tempted to call him, she deleted his number from her cell. Every once in a while, she would find and open the e-mail in which he'd given it to her. Sometimes she would dial part of his number, but she always put the phone down before she completed it. By now he had moved on and found someone else to rape and she was sure she was at best a pleasant memory of the few good times they'd had together.

"Ms. Aaronson:"
Linda shut the e-mail from Sylvia without reading the rest. A message from her boss that started with her last name in the greeting could contain nothing positive. She decided to read it after lunch. She ignored the large

smoked Gouda, tomato, and avocado sandwich on sourdough that Jason had left for her and opened a can of tomato soup. She'd lost thirty pounds in the last three months and couldn't remember the last time she'd worked out. Her skin hung in flaps and folds and she couldn't blame Jason for not wanting to make love to her. If Phil saw her now, he probably would be repulsed as well. Even her breasts had shrunk so her bras gaped uncomfortably and she'd taken to wearing tank tops under her blouses and sweaters.

When she returned to the office, Linda knew she really had no reason to read Sylvia's e-mail. Instead, she pulled out a piece of vellum stationary from a box on the closet shelf. The ballpoint scratched across the paper, so Linda found a rollerball in the same color.

My dearest Phil,

I miss you so very, very much. My life is incomplete without you. When Jason forced me to pick him or you, I chose to stay with him because we've been together for more than nineteen years, because I couldn't imagine my life without him, because I didn't think you had a place for me in your day-to-day life.

I made the wrong decision. So many wrong choices.

She reached for the tissue box, but it was empty. Of course, that first choice, the decision not to walk away from Phil's massage invitation, was the one that cost her everything. Was destroying her marriage and losing her job worth the price? She wiped her nose on her sleeve. At least she had learned what it was like to be alive, if only for a few months. She picked up the pen.

I should have listened to you and never told Jason in the first place.

The ink had smeared in several places where her tears had dropped onto the paper. She set the letter aside and opened Sylvia's e-mail.

Ms. Aaronson:

The contract you signed when the company agreed to let you work remotely stipulated that you travel to Chicago no less than once every other month. You have not been to the office for four months and refuse to answer any questions about when you will schedule your next trip here.

Unfortunately, as much as I appreciate the excellent job you have done supervising the Customer Service Department, I do not believe you can continue to be an effective manager unless you immediately resume face-to-face interactions with your direct reports, department heads, and other team members.

I understand that your reluctance to travel may be a result of the incident that occurred the last time you were in Chicago and I very much sympathize if that's the case. If you wish to take a leave of absence to obtain counseling, I will support that decision. Of course, if you do that, I can't promise the exact same position will be available to you when you return. However, I will make every effort to help you find something appropriate within the company once you are ready to resume regular visits to Chicago.

Otherwise, it might be best if you sought employment locally. I will be happy to write you a letter of recommendation to facilitate your search.

Please advise me of your decision by the end of the week so I can take whatever action is appropriate.

Sincerely,
Sylvia Feldstein

Linda left the e-mail open on her computer and returned to Phil's letter.

If I could go back and choose differently, I would.

Which choice would she have changed? Did it matter, now?

But I'm stuck with the consequences of the choices I did make. I do hope you can forgive me for making the wrong ones and that you've found other women who will meet your needs.
All my love, Linda.

She waved the paper to dry the wet spots, folded it in thirds, slipped it into an envelope, wrote Phil's address on the front, then rummaged around in her desk drawer for a stamp.

Extracting her driver's license from her wallet, Linda zipped it into the pocket of her rain jacket. She tucked the letter in another pocket and paused in the doorway for a moment before locking the handle and pulling the door closed. Zipping up the jacket that draped around her with almost enough room for another person, she marched to Third Street and deposited the envelope in a blue postal box. With her jacket hood pulled down to her eyes, she trudged up the slope to the Burnside Bridge, vaguely aware of the dingy storefronts and the homeless clustering out of the rain in doorways of social service agencies.

Halfway between the two towers, Linda stopped and leaned against the wet railing. Shivering in the wind, she looked over and stared at the darkness below, vaguely aware of the water flowing underneath the bridge.

"Just get it over with." The sound of her own voice startled her, but she was right. She unzipped her jacket and tied it to the railing.

CHAPTER TWENTY-ONE

"What's wrong Phil?" Carol ran one finger the length of his arm.

Phil shook his head and glanced at the clock. He'd spaced out for at least fifteen minutes. "Linda. I haven't heard from her since her husband engineered her birthday surprise then threw me out two days later." He reached over the counter for the coffeepot and refilled his cup. "She hasn't been to Chicago since, and I'm worried about her. I've even heard rumors that Mark's going to be promoted into her job."

He looked at his still black coffee and sighed. "When she thought Jason would accept her relationship with me, she was ecstatic. I'm afraid going back to the way things were, essentially giving up sex, could devastate her."

Carol handed him the cream pitcher. "Sex isn't everything."

He sighed. "Not to you and certainly not to Jason. But, she and I have extremely high libidos. We need sex, a lot of sex."

She put a hand on his arm. "I know. Have you started looking for a new secondary?"

He shook his head. "I keep hoping. I know I'll never find someone as exquisitely compatible sexually."

Her hand slipped down to his thigh. "I guess you're just stuck with me in the interim."

He grinned. "I could think of worse fates." He leaned over close enough so his lips hovered near hers. She closed the gap and pressed her mouth to his. He parted his lips and she slid her tongue between them. Phil waited until she took his hand and placed it on her breast before he slid off the barstool and embraced her.

Carol pressed her hips against him. They both were breathing heavily. His lips drifted from her mouth along her neck to the cleavage exposed by her black lace nightgown. He stayed alert to her reaction, careful not to move too quickly, always waiting for her signal that she was ready to proceed to the next level.

Taking his hand, Carol led him back to the bed they'd abandoned only an hour before. He lay on his back and opened his arms. She knelt beside him, hesitated, then stretched out on top of him, pressing her small breasts against his chest. Gently he caressed her firm ass, easing the silky nightgown up to her waist.

Eventually, she raised herself up on her knees and positioned herself over his cock. He pressed his lips together, resisting the urge to grab her hips and slam himself up into her hot, moist folds. Instead he waited for the inevitable hesitation before she eased herself down. He watched her face change from grimace to neutral to pleasure. Only then did she move. Only then did he lightly rest one hand on her hip, diddling her clit with his other thumb.

She leaned forward to kiss him and he slid his hand from her hips to her breast, massaging it gently, tweaking the nipple with his thumb. He pushed away thoughts of Linda, how she would have come four times by now, how her full breasts would have pressed against his chest, how he could bite her nipples and pinch her ass.

Phil watched Carol's face, looking for the line between her eyebrow that formed when she got close, then increased the pressure on her clit. He pushed up into her downstroke, just enough to bump up the tension on his cock so he could orgasm with her. Once she came, she only wanted to cuddle and if he came first, no amount of stroking could bring her off unless he left the room. In the five years they'd been lovers, she hadn't been able to get over her aversion to oral.

After their climax, Phil held Carol in his arms and ran his fingers gently through her hair. He knew he'd still have to jerk off to rape fantasy porn once she left for the swing shift at the hospital. He sighed. "I'd better get to work."

Jason stopped at Dan & Louis' for a Captain's Platter in hopes of enticing Linda to eat. She'd lost so much weight pining for her lover, all her luscious plump curves had dissolved away. He knew she would leave him for Phil eventually, but he still felt obligated to take care of her until she realized she had stayed with the wrong man.

The condo was dark when he arrived. He looked for Linda in her office, in the loft upstairs, and on both decks. She hadn't left, her suitcases still occupied the top shelf of the upstairs hall closet, none of her clothes were missing, and her purse sat on her desk. Since the computer was still on, he hit the space bar and the screen lit up with an open e-mail. Hoping for a clue, he scanned it, his chest tightening, his eyes watering.

Jason fell into the desk chair. Linda had worked for the same company her entire career, longer then they'd been married. Her job was the most important thing in her life. Until this moment he would have guessed it more important than their marriage, except she hadn't traveled to Chicago because of him.

Where would she go? He thought about calling Phil, but how could she have traveled to Seattle without even her purse? Her cell phone sat next to the mouse and he scanned through the call log. Nothing in the past two days, and the calls before that were all from or to him or work numbers.

He called Melinda and then Joanne, but neither had spoken to Linda in months. They both tried to find out what was going on, but he cut them off with promises to let them know when he learned something.

Jason debated between going out to look for Linda and staying home in case she returned. He now empathized with all the times in the past few months that she must have waited and worried, wondering when he would come home. But, he always did. He ate some of the fried fish and stashed the more tempting delicacies in the fridge.

When he couldn't keep his eyes open, Jason stretched out on the sofa, hoping he would wake when Linda came through the front door. Instead, daylight creeping in between the curtains brightened the living room, nudging him back to consciousness. He ran upstairs, maybe Linda had snuck in while he slept.

Their bed hadn't been touched.

The landline jangled and his heart jumped to his throat. They only kept the bloody thing for emergencies and almost no one had the number. Because it was unlisted, they didn't even get sales or polling calls. Jason dashed back downstairs to the office. Trembling, he picked up the handset. "Hello?"

"May I speak to Linda Aaronson, please"

"She's not here right now. This is her husband, may I help you?"

"Mr. Aaronson, this is Sgt. Baker of the Portland Police Department.

Can you tell me if your wife has lost her driver's license or if there's any possibility it could have been stolen?"

I guess DMV would have the number. Jason took a deep breath and held the phone against his shoulder with his chin so he could extract Linda's red leather wallet from her purse. "Her license isn't in her wallet where she usually keeps it. Why?"

"Could you have her stop by the Central Precinct as soon as possible?"

"Sergeant, please tell me what's going on? I don't know where my wife is. She never came home last night, I haven't seen her since yesterday morning. Before then, she hadn't left our condo in weeks and I found an e-mail that reads as if her boss has fired her."

Jason got no response for what seemed like several minutes, but the line didn't go dead. "Hello? Hello?"

"Mr. Aaronson, are you at home now?"

"Yes."

"You still live on Naito Parkway?"

"Yes."

"If you will please stay there, I'll send an officer over right away."

"Please. I'm begging you. Tell me what's going on."

"I'll have an officer there within ten minutes." The line went dead.

Jason stumbled into the kitchen, grabbed a soda from the fridge, swallowed half of it to wake himself up, then put his jacket back on. He fumbled with his keys until he could lock the door and staggered down the stairs to the building entrance.

A squad car pulled up before he could reach the curb and an officer with long blond hair in a ponytail and round gold studs in her ears lowered the window as he approached.

"Please, Ma'am, can you tell me what's going on? Do you know anything about what might have happened to my wife?"

"Mr. Aaronson?"

Jason nodded.

"I'm sorry, sir, I don't have any information, I've just been asked to give you a ride to the Central Precinct. If you'll get in..."

Jason dashed out into the street and didn't hear whatever else she might have said. She reached over and opened the passenger door. He jumped in and buckled his seat belt. Never having ridden in a police car before, not knowing what to do or say, he just stared at his hands folded in his lap until the officer stopped the car and turned the key. She led him through an empty corridor into a small room containing only a metal table and four chairs. "If you have a seat, sir, I'll let Sgt. Baker know you're here."

Dropping into one of the chairs, Jason clasped his hands together on the table and watched the door. A burly fellow at least six feet tall, carrying a manila folder, entered and extended his hand. "Mr. Aaronson, I'm Sgt. Baker."

Jason didn't unclasp his hands. He stared at the officer. "Where's my wife?"

Sgt. Baker sat across from Jason, set a manila folder on the table, and handed Jason a square piece of plastic. "We found this in a woman's extra large, green, Columbia jacket tied to a railing on the Burnside Bridge."

Jason stared at the tiny photo of Linda, thirty pounds ago, smiling so her full cheeks were visible. He placed the license on the table in front of his chair, squaring it up with the edge. "Do you have the jacket? I think it's Linda's," he whispered.

The sergeant cleared his throat. "We didn't make the connection at the time, but about an hour and a half ago we pulled a Jane Doe from the Willamette River, just downstream from the Steel Bridge."

Jason gripped the edge of the table.

"No one reported a jumper off either bridge and the body was of a woman much smaller than listed there," the sergeant tapped the license with his index finger, "or who could wear the jacket we found that in." He cleared his throat again. "As you might know Mr. Aaronson, most women are less than honest about the weight they list on their driver's licenses, but they usually remove pounds rather than add them."

"She's lost a lot of weight, recently." Jason bit his lip. Linda wouldn't commit suicide just because she lost her job. *But, losing her job on top of losing Phil, on top of his neglect.* He closed his eyes.

The sergeant opened the folder and pushed an eight by ten photograph across the table. "I'm sorry to ask you to do this, Mr. Aaronson, but can you identify the body we pulled from the river in this photograph?"

Jason didn't want to open his eyes. If he didn't look, it couldn't be her. But, he couldn't stop himself from peeking. The face in the photograph was bloated almost beyond recognition. Almost. He put his hand over his mouth to suppress the sob that threatened to well up from his gut.

"You don't have to say anything, Mr. Aaronson. Just please nod if that's your wife."

Jason lifted his chin half an inch and let it fall to his chest.

"Is there anyone you'd like me to call?"

Jason turned his head an inch in each direction.

"Do you want to see a member of the clergy?"

Again, Jason shook his head.

"We're going to need to interview you about your wife's mental state, Mr.

Aaronson. And, of course there's paperwork you'll need to fill out to claim her body. But, there was no sign of foul play. According to the preliminary report from the coroner, the injuries were consistent with someone jumping off a bridge into the river." The sergeant placed a business card next to the driver's license and replaced the photograph in the folder. "I'll let you stay here until you're able to speak with us or can tell us who you would like us to contact. We can take care of the reports a bit later."

Jason heard the door close and put his arms on the table, resting his forehead on the cold, metal top. *I killed her. It's all my fault.* Once the sobs started, he couldn't stop them. His shoulders shook and his tears pooled up under his face. Nausea overcame him, but he hadn't eaten breakfast and had nothing in his stomach to expel. Only when he felt wrung out and completely dry did he lift his head. A box of tissues stood in the middle of the table that he didn't remember seeing before. The room was still empty, the door closed. He blew his nose, wiped his eyes, and then blew his nose again.

Slowly he pushed against the table until he could stand, waiting a moment to feel steady enough on his feet to walk across the room to the trash can and deposit the wad of used tissues. Returning to the table, he sat back down and dialed the number on the business card.

"Sgt. Baker, Central Precinct."

Jason's voice came out in a hoarse squeak. "If I could get a glass of water, I believe I can take care of the paperwork now."

Jason debated with himself for hours whether or not to tell Phil about the funeral. When he put Linda's phone on the charger so he could find the man's number, he noticed seven missed calls all from an unidentified Seattle number starting two days after... he couldn't even think the word. He couldn't find Phil's number in Linda's contacts and he'd deleted it from his own history. He dialed the mystery number from his own cell phone.

"Jason? Is everything okay. I got the strangest letter from Linda and she hasn't returned my phone calls or e-mails."

Jason swallowed. "I guess Sylvia didn't tell you? She's gone."

"Gone where? When will she back?"

Jason gripped the arm of the desk chair so hard he felt it crack. "She jumped off the Burnside Bridge Monday," he said through gritted teeth. All he heard at the other end of the line was the sharp intake and exhalation of breath. "I didn't know if you wanted to come to the funeral. If you do it's Saturday at eleven o'clock, River View Cemetery Funeral Home. You can Google it." He disconnected the call, set the phone on Linda's desk, and buried his face in his arms.

CHAPTER TWENTY-TWO

So many details. Jason spent the days after the trip to the police station consumed by details. Making funeral arrangements, getting his suit cleaned, changing the bank accounts, stopping her subscriptions, turning off her phone, canceling the doctor's appointment he'd finally persuaded her to make, stopping his prescription, sending his lesson plans and final exam to the substitute Richard had hired to teach his classes for the last three weeks of the term.

Every time he crawled into bed, he thought of someone else he should have contacted or told about the funeral. He took to keeping a pad of paper and a pencil on the nightstand, because he forgot who they were by morning.

When he woke up to find dawn peaking between the curtains at five thirty Saturday morning, he was relieved it was almost over.

He had set the alarm for seven thirty. Jason used the extra time to mix up an additional batch of cookies — oatmeal raisin to go with the chocolate chip, snickerdoodles, and ginger snaps he had baked the day before. He really didn't think anyone would come to the condo after the funeral, assuming anyone showed up for that, but it gave him something to do. He'd also made three kinds of dip and bought corn, potato, and vegetable chips. If nothing else, he could eat himself into a junk food coma after he returned from the funeral home. Healthy junk food, made with organic whole grain everything, but junk food none the less.

Jason's cell phone beeped out the seven-thirty alarm he had set just as he pulled the last tray of cookies out of the oven. He left them to cool and went upstairs to shower and dress. Before leaving, he arranged platters of cookies, bowls of chips, glasses, plates and napkins on the counter, leaving room for the bowls of dips and bottles of soda in the refrigerator. He stuck the cookie sheets and cooling racks back into the oven to get them out of the way.

Rather than risk driving, he walked the half mile to the bus stop and took the number thirty-five. The funeral director had offered to send a car, but he saw no reason to pay the extra money. Every time he passed by a planter or hanging basket filled with blooming flowers, he cringed. Linda loved Spring so very much. She would point out the glorious colors whenever they passed them and drag him to the various gardens around town to enjoy the visual feast.

By the time the bus dropped him off a block from the funeral home, he had dampened the first of the five handkerchiefs he had stuffed in various pockets.

As he expected, the room was empty when he arrived. Linda's plain, pine casket was draped with a white cloth and the bouquet of red roses he'd purchased was fanned across one end. He stared from the doorway, unable to enter. Once he burned her body, he would have to admit that he would never see her again, never hold her, never see her smile when he made something she loved to eat, never sit across from her at a restaurant, never hear her moan or cry out when he made her come. He fumbled in his pants pocket for the second handkerchief.

"Mr. Aaronson, you're early." The funeral director — Jason couldn't remember her name — stood at his elbow. "You're welcome to go in, of course, but you asked for an eleven o'clock service and it's only nine-forty-five."

Jason pulled his cell phone from his pocket and checked the time. He shrugged. "Guess I misjudged how long it would take to get here." He almost asked if he could just get it over with, but then if someone did show up they'd be disappointed.

The director took his arm and guided him to a chair in the front row. "You're welcome to stay here until the service. Would you like a cup of coffee?"

He nodded.

"Cream or sugar?"

He shook his head.

Jason held the paper cup in both hands until the coffee was lukewarm. Not knowing what else to do, he drank it just to get rid of it and set the empty cup down on the chair next to his.

At ten thirty he went to the restroom, afraid if he didn't the coffee would come back to haunt him during the service. Washing his hands, he stared at the gaunt, haggard face in the mirror wondering who it belonged to. Not until he watched himself splash cold water on his skin did he realize that it was his own. "Alone. I'm all alone and I will be for whatever's left of my life," he told his reflection. The best he could hope for was an early demise.

When he returned to the room, he was surprised to see half the chairs were occupied. He recognized Richard from the back and two couples sitting together looked like Melinda and Joanne with their husbands. As he walked down the aisle, nodding to those he knew, several faces looked unfamiliar, but the *Oregonian* had updated the lurid details of Linda's suicide with a notice about the service. No telling who might have seen that.

Phil sat at one end of the front row. Jason had to admit his rival's face looked worse than his own. *Aren't we a pair? Couple of juveniles who destroy something we both covet rather than share it.* Except Phil had been willing to share, Jason was forced to remind himself as he took his seat. He and he alone was responsible for causing Linda to take her life. Not only wouldn't he share her with Phil, but when she didn't do as he expected and run after her lover, he punished her by making sure she regretted her decision.

Jason sat with his hands in his lap, his chin on his chest, while the funeral director officiated. Melinda and Joanne both got up and said what he was sure were nice things. So did a woman named Rosie and man named Jonathon, but Jason never heard them say what their connection to Linda was. He wasn't sure which he found more comforting — that he wasn't expected to speak or that Phil didn't get up to say anything. He realized the service was over when the funeral director explained that the cremains would be given to Jason at a later time and everyone was invited to stop by the condo.

Crap, how am I supposed to get home before all these people arrive?

"I drove down, Dude." Phil put a hand on his shoulder. "Can I give you a lift?"

"Thanks." Jason hoped Phil wasn't a mind reader. Although he was willing to admit his responsibility for Linda's death to himself, he certainly didn't want to share that fact with anyone else.

He followed Phil out to a blue Acura in the parking lot and climbed into the passenger seat. When Phil turned onto Macadam, Jason said. "I'm sorry."

"Later, Dude. You and I can, *should,* talk later." He moved over to the left lane. "You still need to get through the visitation."

Jason showed Phil the guest parking spot and he followed Jason to the apartment. While Jason put out the bowls of dip and stashed the covers in the oven with the cookie sheets, Phil opened the curtains and turned on all the lights. Jason had just pulled the last bottle from the fridge when the doorbell rang. Phil opened it to admit Melinda and her husband. He left the door ajar and everyone else entered without knocking.

Jason busied himself passing cookies, refilling drinks, and pouring more chips into half empty bowls. The people filling his condo seemed content to talk amongst themselves, although occasionally someone put a hand on his bicep or an arm around his shoulder. Melinda was the first to say good-bye, apologizing because she had to drive to Corvallis to attend a lecture at Oregon State. Her departure started an exodus, and by two thirty the condo was empty except for him and Phil.

So much for a junk food coma. Jason stared at the ravaged counter. Only a few cookies, some chip crumbs at the bottom of the large bowls, and the dip that clung to the sides of the smaller ones remained. Phil was collecting plates and glasses that he found scattered around on tables and bookshelves so Jason loaded them into the dishwasher. When he started it, Phil piled the remaining dishes in the sink and took a dish rag around to wipe up moisture left behind on glass and laminate furniture. Jason remembered the lids, cookies sheets, and cooling racks he'd stashed in the oven, pulled them out and stood them on end next to the stack of dishes.

When they'd finished tidying up, Phil opened the closet and rummaged in his coat pocket, emerging with a bottle of single malt. He set it on the counter and Jason hand washed two of the highball glasses awaiting the next dishwasher load. Phil poured the amber liquid until each glass was half full. Jason took a sip. *Don't need to worry any more about mixing alcohol with sildenafil citrate.* The liquor went down smoothly, too smoothly. He tipped the glass and swallowed repeatedly until it was empty. The burn spread from his mouth to his stomach and bathed his brain, numbing the thoughts that had taunted him for his failures this past week.

Phil refilled both glasses and handed Jason's back to him. With one hand he guided Jason by the elbow over to the sofa while transporting the bottle and his own glass in the other. He set the bottle on the table and held his glass out for Jason to clink. "To Linda," he said before gulping down the contents.

"To Linda." Jason did the same, grateful for the numbing effect of the alcohol. "I killed her because I was selfish."

Phil punched his upper arm. "Didja throw her off the bridge?"

Jason shook his head. He held his glass out to Phil, then thought better of it and set it on the table. "She begged me not to make her choose, but I couldn't stand sharing her. She'd been my wife for almost two decades. I couldn't cope with the thought of her in another man's arms then coming home to our bed."

"Selfish." Phil poured more scotch in the two glasses and offered Jason one.

Jason shook his head. "Figured she'd choose you, move to Seattle, and leave me. Thought I'd sell the condo and find a way..." He put his head in his hands and sobbed. "I'd rather she had. It'd be better knowing she was with you than this..."

Phil pulled Jason's head against his shoulder and let Jason bawl, soaking his shirt. "She had other choices. Suicide wasn't her only option."

When Jason finally sat back up, sniveling, Phil looked at him. "Dude, one thing I just don't get. Why in the world would you think she would choose me? Did you ever see how that woman looked at you? She adored you."

Jason shook his head. "I saw how she looked at you." He jabbed a finger into Phil's upper arm. "She'd fallen in love with you."

"I know. I fell in love with her too. But, she never stopped loving you. She never wanted to hurt you."

Jason picked up the glass Phil had poured earlier and emptied it. "What the hell have I done?"

Phil put a hand on his shoulder. "Tried to live by other people's rules, even when they didn't work for you or, especially, for your wife."

Jason woke up on top of the bed. He didn't remember passing out, or how he'd gotten upstairs. He was wearing everything he'd had on for the funeral except his jacket and shoes. The clock said one fifteen, but it was pitch black so he had to assume it was a.m. not p.m. His stomach roiled and he realized what had woken him. Pushing himself off the bed, he managed to make it to the bathroom, flip on the light and lift the toilet lid before his stomach purged itself.

After he rinsed his mouth and splashed cold water on his face, he looked up to see Phil standing in the doorway with a glass of dark liquid. "Cola? You'll feel better."

Jason sat down on the toilet lid and wept, holding his head in his hands. "Linda..." he wailed.

Phil set the glass on the corner of the vanity and disappeared. When his tears subsided, Jason downed the now-lukewarm cola and hiccupped. He washed his face and returned to the bed.

The next time he opened his eyes, enough sunlight penetrated the curtains to make his head hurt. Downstairs he found Phil eating a sandwich, standing over the sink. He rinsed the crumbs off his fingers. "Feel up to eating?"

Jason shook his head. "I just wanted to ask you if you wanted something, of Linda's, a memento?"

"A picture would be nice. Never got to take any." Phil put the mustard jar back in the fridge.

Jason pulled a photo album from the bookcase and sat down on the sofa.

Phil stood behind him as he flipped through the pages. "None of those photographs do her justice. Her beauty was her exuberance for life and love. Those made her eyes and skin shine in a way a camera could never capture." He leaned over and pointed to a photograph of Linda leaning down to smell a rose.

Surrounded by bushes of yellow, pink, red, and white flowers, she looked at the camera and her smile lit her eyes. It hurt to see her so happy and know she would never inhale the fragrance of another flower. Jason snapped the album shut and lifted it over his shoulder. "Here, you can have all of them. Just throw out any with me in them."

"Dude, it hurts to look at them now, but eventually you'll want them to help you remember her. Phil lifted the album out of his hands. "Why don't I take a few, scan them, and mail them back?"

Jason nodded, without looking up. "Okay."

"Appreciate it, Dude. Listen, I gotta get back home. You gonna be okay?"

"Sure."

"You have my number."

"Thanks." Jason waited until he heard the door close then fell over on his side.

CHAPTER TWENTY-THREE

The white ceramic urn with a single red rose painted on it was shaped like a tea or coffee pot without spout or handle. Jason stared at it, unable to accept it from the funeral director's hands. She set it down on the desk in front of him.

"You have several options, Mr. Aaronson. You may take this with you, purchase a crypt for it in the mausoleum, or have it buried in the cemetery."

Jason traced each calligraphed letter of Linda's full name and the numbers framing the years of her life.

"If you wish to take it with you, I can pack it up for you in the box it was shipped here in."

His chin rested on his chest and he couldn't meet her eyes.

"If you'd like to leave it here for a week or two until you decide, we have a thirty-day grace period. After that, we must charge you for storage."

"Thanks," he whispered.

"Also, if there's another relative you'd prefer we send it to..."

Their families had disowned them for marrying outside their religion, a decision they both found laughable since at best they both considered themselves agnostics. Given the repressive relationships they'd had with their parents, neither regretted breaking off contact. He had no one to send her to. "Can I take her with me now and then bring her back for you to ship? I'd like to keep her with me until..."

"Keep the box and all the packing material. If you parcel up the urn properly, you can ship it via the U.S. Postal service. Just be aware that private carriers won't accept cremains." She handed him a brochure. "Do you want me to prepare this for you to take with?"

Jason managed to lift his chin up from his chest far enough to approximate a nod before it dropped back down. He didn't know how long he sat in her office, alone, staring at his hands folded in his lap. Eventually, a box was placed on his legs, forcing him to separate his hands and place one on either side of it.

"You'll want to keep it upright, but if it's tilted or even turned upside down the seal should still hold."

Jason stood, gripping the box tightly against his chest. So light. So little left to remember the beautiful woman who had eloped with him almost twenty years ago. Leaving the funeral home, clutching all that was left of his wife, Jason blinked furiously in the bright sunshine. Whenever he ventured out of doors, he was taken aback by daylight. He expected the world to be clouded in the same gloom that he endured.

After trudging almost half a mile to the bus stop, Jason wished he had chosen to drive. On the one hand, he didn't have to worry about securing the box in a station wagon. On the other, he would have to hold it all the way back into downtown and walk the dozen blocks home. Maybe he should transfer to the thirty three which would drop him off only four blocks from the condo.

By the time the bus arrived, his arms ached from the awkward position. He decided transferring, even if it only saved him eight blocks, would be worth the ten- or fifteen-minute wait. He just didn't have the energy for walking that he did when Linda was alive and he ate three meals a day.

Setting the box between his feet at the top of the steps, he extracted his transit pass. His wife was traveling with him, should he pay for her as well? A tear trickled down his cheek and hung at the end of his chin. Many seats were empty, since it was only one o'clock. He found an unoccupied bench and set Linda down next to the window. She always preferred the window seat.

Struggling aboard the second bus, trying to balance the box while he climbed the steps, Jason regretted not staying on the first one. He couldn't see an empty seat and couldn't decide whether he should hold the box with one hand and a strap with the other or risk putting the box on the floor between his feet so he could hang on properly.

A girl wearing torn black jeans, a laced-up top, and knee-high boots with huge metal buckles stood up and let him have her seat. He felt embarrassed needing to take a seat from a woman, But Linda would have needed a seat and she could sit on his lap.

"Thanks," he said to the woman who had at least five pieces of metal piercing her face, not including dozens hanging from her ears.

She just nodded and grabbed the strap as the bus lurched forward.

At home, Jason sliced open the packing tape with a kitchen knife and lifted Linda from the box. Setting her on the counter, he undressed her and stuffed all the packing material back in the box. Looking around, he tried to decide whether Linda would prefer to sit on the coffee table or the fireplace mantle. The former seemed too low to give her a proper view of the downstairs, and the urn was too wide for the narrow marble ledge above the fireplace. Finally he decided to leave her on the edge of the counter, where she could watch him working at his desk under the stairs, see whoever came in the front door, and keep an eye on anyone trying to get into her office.

He planted a kiss on the cold ceramic. "Welcome back home, darling."

It took Jason a week to work up the courage to empty Linda's closet. He made no attempt to sort things out, just threw everything that would fit into her suitcases and sat on them to zip them up. He retrieved boxes from any store in the neighborhood that would supply them, filled up the car with everything she had worn, and drove it over to Sunshine Division. The supervisor looked at him quizzically. When he explained he was a recent widower, her face softened and she helped him unload the car. He turned down her offer of a receipt and drove back home.

Each time he entered the condo was as difficult as every time before. It never got easier to come home to an empty apartment, knowing he had extinguished all the light and laughter in his life. Sometimes he stood outside with the key in the lock for ten or twenty minutes trying to screw up the courage to open the door.

Sylvia said he didn't have to return the company's computer equipment as long as he wiped the hard drive. He packed it up and took it to Free Geek, along with the printer and the fax machine that Linda hadn't used for years. Powell's bought most of the books. He took cash rather than credit and handed it to the bearded fellow wearing a tattered shirt and shoes not quite attached to the soles who was selling *Street Roots* at the store entrance. He dropped off the rejected books at the central branch on Tenth Street for the next Friends of the Library sale.

Each project sapped all his energy and he required several days to recover. The liquor store became a twice-a-week stop — he needed at least three or four shots to get to sleep at night. He had wondered how Linda, in her last months, had been able to just stop eating, despite his efforts to tempt her with her favorite delicacies. But, once he had consumed everything in the pantry and fridge, the prospect of buying groceries just seemed too much of a bother. If he was out and thought about it, sometimes he grabbed a meal from one of the numerous food carts within blocks of the condo. But everything he ate tasted the same, so he switched to pre-made sandwiches from grocery and convenience stores. If he didn't have another reason to leave the condo, even picking up prepared food was too much trouble.

Jason had to punch another hole in his belts, because without one his pants slid down over his hips. Every time he walked through Old Town, he dropped a bag of his own clothing off at the homeless camp at Fourth and Burnside. After the second visit they recognized him and expressed concern for his welfare. He assured them he'd just lost a lot of weight and wanted to replace everything he had with clothing that fit.

He hired Joanne to sell the condo. She tried to convince him that if he waited six months he might get a better price. Since the mortgage wasn't under water, he assured her that he wanted to get rid of the place sooner rather than later. She sighed and helped him stage the apartment for show-ings, making him pack up some of the knickknacks and other trinkets Linda had decorated the house with. He gave them to the CAT Adoption Team thrift store.

Joanne insisted that Linda couldn't stay on the counter. Jason refused to move her, but agreed to hide her in the upstairs closet whenever Joanne showed the condo to prospective buyers. He stopped shaving so he wouldn't have to worry about hair in the sink and took to sleeping on the sofa every night. He found it much easier to fold up the comforter and put it away than arrange all the little pillows Joanne had acquired for the bed. Besides, the sofa didn't have a conspicuously empty side that taunted him through the night.

Richard called to ask him if he planned to come back to school in the Fall. Jason asked about a leave of absence and Richard said he would look into it. He never called back, which didn't surprise Jason. Since he hadn't finished Spring term, he didn't have tenure. Richard could just avoid re-newing Jason's contract. Phil called a couple of times the first few weeks, but Jason didn't answer. Phil never left a voicemail and the calls stopped a month after Linda's death.

When Joanne telephoned with an offer on the condo, Jason didn't know whether to laugh or cry. He decided neither was appropriate and signed the agreement even though the buyer was offering ten thousand below asking, which was already barely half of what he and Linda had paid. The price would pay off the mortgage with maybe just enough left over to cover the last credit card bill and the post-dated check he'd given the funeral home. Jason celebrated by drinking an entire fifth instead of his usual third of a bottle.

When Joanne told him all the contingencies had been removed, Jason called Community Warehouse and arranged for them to pick up all the furniture, bedding, towels, dishes, electronics and everything else they would take the day before closing. When he closed the door behind them, the only things left in the condo were the fancy pillows Joanne had lent him for staging. He slept on the floor with his head on one of those.

In the morning, he pulled out Linda's stopper and let a bit of her spill out into a plastic sandwich bag. "Hope you don't mind if a little of you stays with me." He replaced the stopper, put tape over it, slipped Linda into a plastic bag, carefully dressed her in bubble wrap, and nestled her in the packing peanuts within the box. After using half a roll of shipping tape to secure the box, he painstakingly wrote the address on the top and all four sides. Before he opened the door, he looked around the empty condo. "Seven years." He patted the box. "We got to live in our dream home for seven years. But, it's time to move on, now. I'm sending you where you should have gone months and months ago. I hope that will work out better for you than I did."

Jason set the box outside the front door while he locked the deadbolt and pocketed the keys. By the time he plodded the six blocks to the post office he was gasping for breath. "I'm out of shape. You don't need some out-of-shape, impotent old man dragging you down," he whispered to Linda.

He had to wait in line for almost twenty minutes and worried that he hadn't allowed enough time. When he set the box on the counter, the clerk looked at him with lips pursed and pointed down.

"Which address is this going to? You're only supposed to have one address on a package."

"They're all the same address." Jason pressed his lips together. If he could take Linda somewhere else he would, but the brochure the funeral director explicitly said only the post office would transport her.

The clerk pulled out a giant marker and blacked out the addresses on the sides of the box. "One per package. You're only supposed to write the address on the package once." She turned the box sideways and Jason winced.

"Return address?"

Jason shook his head. "I don't have one."

"Packages must have a return address. You can use a relative's."

Jason took the market and wrote FROM and the condo address on the top of the box.

The clerk set the box on her scale. "Does this package contain alcohol, prescription drugs, tobacco, handguns, or any hazardous material including perfumes, nail polish, flea collars or flea sprays, aerosols, bleach, pool chemicals, paints, matches..."

"Ashes. It's my wife's ashes." Jason snapped.

"Are they packaged in a silt-proof container?"

He nodded.

"You'll have to send it registered or express mail." The clerk looked at her computer screen. "Registered is..."

Jason handed her the one credit card he hadn't yet cancelled. "Just send it Express Mail."

She pushed a form across to him. "Fill this out, then. Step aside so I can help someone else while you do, but you don't have to get back in line."

Jason sighed and accepted the ballpoint pen she handed him. He moved to one side of the window and filled in all the required information. Since he had written the mailing address down five times, he remembered it and didn't have to consult the piece of paper in his pocket. The package stayed on the scale while the clerk sold stamps to an elderly woman who couldn't decide if she wanted flags or bonsai.

Jason shifted his weight from one foot to the other, looked at the clock on the wall behind the clerk, and confirmed it against the time on his cell phone. Finally the women counted out enough single dollar bills and secured the stamps in her pocketbook. She reminded Jason of his *bubby* and for half a moment he regretted losing touch with his family. He snorted. Not that they'd offer him comfort now, just berate him for marrying a shiksa.

He practically shoved the woman out of the way to step back in front of the clerk. She took his form and wrote CREMAINS and FRAGILE in block letters on two sides above where she had scratched out the address and diagonally across the top. "Return receipt?"

"No, thanks."

She handed him the credit card receipt and his copy of the Express Mail form. He shoved them in his pocket, pushed his way out of the post office, and tore south on Broadway to the bus stop.

When he arrived at the title company offices, Joanne wrinkled her nose. "Jason, have you thought about seeing a grief counselor? When was the last time you bathed?"

He shrugged. "Sorry, forgot to keep a bath towel."

She tilted her head and stared at him, her eyebrows drawn together and her lips pushed out. But, the receptionist escorted them into a conference room, cutting off Joanne's inquiry. For the next hour, she handed him document after document to sign, explaining what each one was and urging him to read them. He just signed and initialed wherever the escrow officer pointed. When he was done, he tossed the keys on the table, grabbed the check, and bolted for the door. "Gotta go." He didn't want to wait and give Joanne a chance to interrogate him.

After the paying off the mortgage, various fees, and the Realtor's commission, the check was less than he had expected. He shrugged and walked over to an ATM to deposit it in his credit union account. Along with the money he'd gotten for the Subaru, it should be enough.

Jason took the bus back downtown and sat at the Max stop, watching the trains disgorge people and fill up again, until the sky darkened. The street lights illuminated the city, as he trudged up the ramp to the Morrison Bridge. As he passed over the water, he thought about duplicating Linda's last act, but the odds of surviving dissuaded him. Instead he walked the length of the bridge to the ramp from the Interstate. By the time he reached the southbound freeway, the roar of the trucks deafened him to all other sounds. The rush of air as each one passed made keeping his footing difficult, but he plodded north until he stood under the east end of the Burnside Bridge.

Jason stopped in the shadows measuring how long it took the trucks to travel from the curve to the north. When he was sure he had the timing down right, he sucked in his breath and stepped across the white line into the traffic lane.

CHAPTER TWENTY-FOUR

Phil brought the pink delivery slip over to the concierge's desk. He'd taken Carol out for some steamed clams at Ivar's before she took the bus up pill hill, so he stood back to avoid overwhelming Raoul with his garlic breath.

"Afternoon, Mr. Walker. Got a package for you." Raoul disappeared into the back room and returned with a box nine inches wide by fifteen inches tall. When he saw "Cremains" in block lettering, Phil found himself unable to step closer to the counter.

"Someone you know, sir?" Raoul tipped the top of the box toward Phil and he recognized Linda's address.

"Someone who shouldn't be here." Gingerly, he accepted the package. "Thanks Raoul."

While waiting for the elevator, Phil examined the box more closely. Big black blotches of marker on all four sides were under the words "Fragile" and "Cremains." Written in block letters, the handwriting was obviously different than that of his address and the address of Linda's condo written across the top of the box.

Phil set the box on the kitchen counter and stepped into his office. A quick search of the Portland newspaper's online site answered his question. He needed a drink. After pouring himself a full glass of single malt, he wandered outside onto the balcony. Leaning on the railing he gazed out over the Sound and sipped at the smoky, ten-year-old scotch.

Two lives gone because he couldn't resist the cherubic face, luscious curves, and insatiable appetite of a monogamously married woman. He closed his eyes. The salty sting of the breeze off the water pricked his skin. He remembered the silky soft feel of Linda's full breasts in his palm, the delicious aroma that emerged from between her legs when he pinched her nipples, the heat of her ass when he spanked her, the decadent taste of her as she came over and over and over again, gushing nectar all over his face. He missed her smile, the sound of her voice on his cell phone, even the ability to discuss CRM database upgrades he'd thought about.

He'd let a local firm lure him away from his old employer to avoid the memories and occasional encounters with Linda's replacement. Mark had moved into her position the Monday after the funeral.

Draining the glass, he debated returning inside to refill it. But, it was early enough in the day he should put in a few more hours work.

Nice guy, Jason. Smart. In another life they might have been friends. He shook his head. No, the only thing they had in common was their love of Linda. And even that worked against them since Jason apparently was one of the brainwashed believers that monogamy was the only relationship option. Assuming Linda had taken his name, he was probably raised Jewish. But, he'd waited almost a week before giving Linda a service and then had cremated her. The man wore leather to the funeral and hadn't covered any of the mirrors in the condo. No mention was made of sitting shiva.

Phil had never seen anything in their home to indicate they subscribed to any Jewish beliefs, no menorah or Star of David decorating the mantle or *Mezuzah* cases on the doors. But even those who abandoned the religions of their youth, whether Christianity or Judaism, clung to the whole monogamy bullshit. He tensed to throw the glass at whatever he could hit, but forced himself to put it on the small round table. He dropped onto the lounger.

Linda had warned him she was married, tried to avoid his advances, pushed him away. But, he had sensed such a yearning in her. She was so sexually frustrated; her deprivation oozed from her pours and beckoned him. Still, in the end she had chosen Jason, knowing he would never satisfy her the way Phil could.

Had Phil given Linda a few months of happiness or destroyed her marriage and her life?

He pushed himself off the chair and stomped back into the house, leaving the door open, fighting the need to slam it hard enough to shatter the glass. Rummaging in his desk, he found a box cutter and clicked out enough of the blade to slice open the tape on the box. Sorting through packing material, he found no note.

Phil lifted the thirteen-inch tall ceramic urn and set it on the wide mahogany fireplace mantle. He shrugged. Actually didn't look that bad there. If not for the inscription it could pass for a piece of art.

He went back to his computer and found the number for River View.

"I'm a friend of Jason Aaronson and wanted to inquire what arrangements had been made."

Phil was put on hold for several minutes then a woman spoke.

"I'm June Liston, the director of the River View. How can I help you?"

Phil repeated himself.

"Do you mind telling me your name, sir?"

"Phil Walker."

"Mr. Walker, I'm glad you called. Mr. Aaronson pre-paid for a cremation, but made no arrangement for services or disposition of the cremains. Under contact information, he listed you as executor of his will, but gave no phone number or address."

Phil sat down, hard. Was this Jason's final revenge, leaving him to sort out the details? Or did the man just have no one else to turn to? Except for his boss and a couple of other professors, most of the people at Linda's funeral appeared to be friends of hers. And, if he'd left his religion behind, he might have abandoned his family as well.

After a long pause, June said: "I'm sorry if you weren't aware of this information, Mr. Walker. To be honest, I have no idea how the legal matters are handled. I just know I have a body and a cremation order, but I don't know if you were planning a funeral service or a memorial."

Phil took a deep breath. He supposed if Jason had made him executor of his will, he'd get official notification eventually and he'd figure out how to find the time to handle the details then. For this decision, the best option was probably to do nothing. If Jason made arrangements for cremation but not a funeral, he probably didn't give a hoot. Phil doubted if anyone would show up anyway. Funerals were designed to comfort the living, and there was no one left to console. Except for a tinge of guilt, Phil was ambivalent about Jason's death and he had already, mostly, mourned Linda's passing.

"Can you send me the cremains and I'll make arrangements for a memorial service?"

"Certainly." The woman sounded relieved. Phil gave her his address.

"Starting a new hobby, Mr. Walker?" Raoul asked when Phil approached the counter, pink notification slip in hand. Raoul disappeared and returned with a box. Although half the size of the one Linda's remains had arrived in, it still had a tag with the word "Cremains" taped next to the shipping label.

Phil scowled at Raoul and accepted the package. It weighed much less as well and he noticed no "Fragile" label.

"Sorry, sir. Didn't mean to offend."

Phil shrugged and carried the box to the elevator. Inside his apartment, he sliced open the package and found it contained a plain, black box and a receipt showing that Jason had pre-paid for his cremation, including ten dollars for his box. "Three-hundred-dollar urn for your wife, ten dollar paper box for yourself? Dude, she loved you as much as you did her."

Phil sat down on the sofa with Linda's urn upside down between his legs. He ripped off the tape and pulled out the stopper. Using a wide mouth funnel, he carefully poured Jason's ashes in with Linda's. He had to hold the stopper in and shake the urn down several times, but he managed to empty the box and ease the stopper all the way back in.

He looked up to see Carol leaning in the doorway of the bedroom watching him.

He put the urn back on the fireplace mantle. Since the box said it was biodegradable on the bottom, he tossed it in the recycle bin.

"At least we won't have two urns on the mantle. That might have been a bit macabre." She walked over and put her arms around his waist.

He hugged her back. Carol had seen him through Gina's death and now Linda's. He stroked her hair. If Linda had left Jason, could they have made things work? She and Carol were as different as he and Jason. *Damn, I would have figured something out, woman, if you'd given me a chance. But you wouldn't leave the man who put his own needs above yours.*

Three weeks later during the first rainy days in September, Phil poured the contents of the urn into four, heavy-duty, gallon-sized, plastic bags.

"You want me to go with you?" Carol wore a light blue rain suit and galoshes. "I don't have a shift this afternoon."

"No, this is something I should do myself. Besides, you never even met them." He put the four plastic bags inside a cloth grocery bag.

"You barely knew Jason."

"I'm doing this for Linda."

He drove down to Portland and met with the lawyer who had drawn up Jason's will. He walked out of the man's office grateful that Jason had left so little for him to do. A few phone calls, a check or two, and he'd be able to dispose of all of his executor duties except one.

Driving west on Highway 26 took much longer than he'd expected, but then he shouldn't have tried to get there during rush hour. He pulled into Washington Park on the west edge of Portland as the rain clouds darkened and the hint of sun in the west disappeared. The parking lot was practically empty and the store had already closed when he pulled into the Rose Garden lot. Before opening the car door, he zipped up his Gore-Tex jacket, pulled the hood over his head, and retrieved the cloth bag from the back seat. He stuffed one of the plastic bags with Linda's and Jason's combined cremains into each of the front pockets of his jacket. Armed with a scissors, he climbed out of the car and stepped out into the drizzle.

Crossing the asphalt, he stood in the dim light with rows and rows of roses — thousands of bushes — extending in either direction. He looked around to make sure he was alone, pulled out the first bag and cut off one corner. Holding it at his hip, he strolled up and down rows until the contents had all sifted out onto the muddy ground. By daylight, the rain would have mixed the ashes with the soil and no one would be the wiser. He cut open the second bag.

When Phil returned to his car, his shoes sloshed, his jeans were soaked to his skin, and his jacket hung heavy on his shoulders. He covered the leather seat with towels, tossed the jacket in the trunk, and climbed in out of the rain. Mission accomplished.

He maneuvered the car back out toward the highway.

Cold, wet, and afraid he would have trouble staying awake driving all the way back to Seattle, Phil passed up the exit toward the freeway northbound and took Highway 26 back through the city, stopping at Stumptown on Third. Sitting at the bar, nursing a triple shot, he watched a voluptuous woman in an ankle-length, black trench coat order a French press.

She planted herself on the barstool next to his and one hand manipulated the keyboard on her phone while the other brought her mug to her full lips. Need radiated off her in waves, exactly the way Linda's deprivation had resonated with him. He stared at the large diamond solitaire and the plain gold band encircling her left ring finger.

Phil emptied his cup and headed for the men's room. When he emerged, he rushed through the shop, ignoring all the other patrons, and pushed his way through the glass doors, bracing himself for the wet chill. Once in his car, he turned up the heat and headed north for the Broadway Bridge, avoiding both the Burnside and the Morrison.

ACKNOWLEDGEMENTS

This book would not have reached your hands without the help of many dear friends and colleagues. I thank my readers and supporters, especially Deborah Dixon, first reader extraordinaire, and M.K. Blackwind who captured the photograph of the Burnside Bridge used to create the cover and illustrate the chapter beginnings. Thanks always and especially to my beloved submissive, Patrick, for his love, his support, his service, and his design skills.

OTHER NOVELS BY KORIN I. DUSHAYL INCLUDE:

BROKEN

Some things can never be fixed

Given a choice between slavery and ostracization, Jessica chooses to kneel naked before her department head so she can continue studying for her PhD in psychology. That decision takes her down a dark path to abuse, exploitation, and torment of both her body and her spirit.

Korin I. Dushayl "writes with authority and compassion about those who live within the lifestyle. Broken and Shattered explore issues including finding and initiating a submissive partner, informed consent, and the difference between dominating someone and exploiting their needs."

Elizabeth Coldwell
author, anthologist, magazine editor

Buy it in Print

or

E-Book

http://www.transgressivewriter.com/broken.php

SHATTERED

Just where do you cross the point of no return?

When a sweet, intelligent twenty-five year old with undiagnosed Aspers-er and PTSD seeks help from a ruthless, unscrupulous, sadistic therapist, she shatters his psyche and throws him into a suicidal depression. Her crude attempt to pick up the pieces — enslaving him and subjecting him to unethical, unsanctioned, experiments — ignores the lines of consent and the responsibilities of a Dominant. — Inspired by a true story.

"The work ... unfolds with the assured touch of a bestselling mainstream author, seducing us into the lives of people with needs and agendas that find wings in the dark. Only an author familiar with this landscape could peel back these layers of psychological complexity without flinching and without dramatic compromise ... Prepare to submit to this reading experi-ence, which will mark you with its narrative power.

Larry Brooks, USA Today bestselling author of
Darkness Bound and *Bait and Switch*

Buy it in Print

or
E-Book

http://www.transgressivewriter.com/shattered.php

PLAYING WITH DOLLS

*"a must read for anyone who ever had
to learn how to be comfortable in their own skin"*

Jesse enjoys playing with dolls and wearing girls' clothing and everyone from his parents, teachers, friends and neighbors assumes he will grow up gay. As an adult the burden of those assumptions hampers his ability to come to terms with his sexuality"

Korin I. Dushayl "has accomplished something remarkable here, crafting a story that works on all levels — educating, arousing, inspiring, empowering, and (most importantly) emotionally connecting with the reader."

Sally Bibrary, Bending the Bookshelf

Buy it in Print

or
E-Book

http://www.transgressivewriter.com/dolls.php

FOR MORE INFORMATION VISIT
TRANSGRESSIVEWRITER.COM

www.ingramcontent.com/pod-product-compliance
Lightning Source LLC
Chambersburg PA
CBHW050749250626
47155CB00005B/1982